SOMEBODY HAS TO LOSE

When American Private Investigator Mark Preston had been sent to find a wealthy missing girl he thought it would take a long time, but he got lucky fast. Then his luck started to run out with shady characters around like Barney Stillman, the tough club-owner, two high-class hoodlums who Preston nicknamed Laurel and Hardy, and Grover J. Mitchell, the president of Art-World Incorporated. But as possible compensation, Louise Carrington was a sight to behold . . .

SOMEBODY HAS TO LOSE

Peter Chambers

·BLACK·
DAGGER
·CRIME·

First published 1975
by
Robert Hale & Company

This edition 2004 by BBC Audiobooks Ltd
published by arrangement with
the author

ISBN 1 4056 8500 X

British Library Cataloguing in Publication Data available

Printed and bound in Great Britain by
Antony Rowe Ltd., Chippenham, Wiltshire

SOMEBODY HAS TO LOSE

PRELUDE

THE orange flasher of the police car appeared round the corner at the bay end of the street. Seconds later the blue and white sedan screeched to a halt outside the apartment building. It was one o'clock in the morning. Two officers climbed out, slamming doors. They stared up at the dark concrete pile, nodded to each other and went inside.

A man detached himself from the shadows and walked rapidly away. Harvey Nelson pressed the elevator button marked fourteen. He was twenty-three years old, a tall blond young man with one year of service in the Monkton City Police Department. He had already been involved in more fights and gun battles than most men would see in a lifetime. His partner was Lou Ritter, a squat, embittered man of thirty. Some of the men on the squad had commiserated with Nelson when he was assigned to Ritter. But Nelson soon learned that when the going was rough, the older man's courage and experience were things to be admired and learned from.

"What do you make of this one, Lou?"

Ritter shrugged, shifting his gun holster.

"We'll soon find out."

They stepped out at fourteen, looking at the numbered arrows on the corridor wall. Apartment 1421 was to the left. They made their way quietly until they reached the apartment next door. Ritter pointed to himself then forward. Nelson nodded. The senior man was indicating that he would go to the far side of the door. They drew their blue-black police issue automatics and took up positions. Nelson pushed the plastic buzzer and they waited. Nothing. He tried again, with the same result. He tried the handle and the door was open. Inside was darkness and silence, but that didn't necessarily mean anything. Nelson slid his left hand inside, feeling up the wall for the light switch, and found it. After he had put the light on, they waited again.

Still nothing.

Ritter nodded and they went in fast and crouching, kicking the door wide before them. Then stopped, together.

"Christ!" muttered Nelson.

Even Lou Ritter was shaken.

The place was like a slaughterhouse. There was blood everywhere, and what remained of the body of a naked woman lay on the floor.

Nelson turned to his partner.

8

"Lou," he began, then turned his head quickly away and retched violently.

"It's okay, kid."

Ritter stepped carefully through the shambles and searched the other rooms. Satisfied that they were alone, he put his gun away and returned to the shaking Nelson.

"Snap out of it, Harve, we got work to do."

He picked up the telephone and dialled.

First to arrive were the medics, but they could do little until the photographer had finished his work, so they stood around smoking and trying not to look at the floor.

Then came the big guns. Lieutenant Rourke of Homicide and his partner Detective Sergeant Gil Randall. The photographer followed. The detectives stared at the scene for a long moment.

"What do you think, Gil?" asked Rourke.

Randall licked his lips.

"Hollings Street," he replied.

Rourke nodded in agreement. They had witnessed an almost identical scene some eighteen months previously. There had been no leads on that one. Maybe they'd have better luck this time. He looked across at Ritter.

"Anything, Lou?"

"No, lieutenant. Nelson and me got the buzz. We came up here and that's all."

"O.K. Better write it up and get back on patrol."

Rourke noted the alacrity with which Ritter's partner made his exit. A rough one for a young fellow like that.

9

The photographer had finished now, and the cleaning up was in progress.

"Better get the manager out of bed, will you Gil? This looks like being a long night."

1

So FAR, it hadn't been too busy a day. I'd spent about an hour watching the girls down on the street from my office window. My fingernails had needed filing, say ten minutes. There'd been some coffee that needed drinking, and once, just for the exercise, I'd walked over to the water cooler and helped myself to a cup of that. Of course, there was the mail to attend to, always a high spot. A man wanted to take ten pounds off my middle in seven days. Some outfit in Kansas offered a shark-hunting expedition, success guaranteed, one thousand dollars inclusive for the whole week. My geography has never been strong, but I would have thought sharks to be somewhat rare in Kansas, even at a thousand smackers a throw. Somebody who called himself a doctor wanted to give me his personal advice about my sex difficulties. There

11

were others too, and the waste paper basket was doing good business.

All this executive work was beginning to exhaust me, so I took a few minutes off to peek at the *Monkton Herald*. There was horse-racing out at Palmtrees today, and one or two of the nags looked promising. A man shouldn't spend his whole life chained to an office desk. Maybe I ought to take a few hours off, and get over there and teach the bookies a lesson. That was when the card came. It said Anthony J. Holford, Attorney-at-law. Mr Holford, it seemed, hung up his shingle in Waldron, a city about a hundred miles north. Inwardly, I groaned. It looked as though the bookies were not going to take that beating today.

He was tallish, about fifty years old, and very dignified. His handshake was firm and dry, and I invited him to take a seat.

"What can I do for you, Mr Holford?"

He cleared his throat.

"I must emphasize, Mr Preston, that this matter is highly confidential."

I nodded.

"Most of my business comes into that category, Mr Holford. And I've been in business for quite some time."

It was his turn to nod.

"Yes, I know. You have been highly recommended by sources in this city."

I wondered who the sources were. Not that I had any quibble with their judgement.

"My client is a most prominent man, most prom-

12

inent. It is important that his name is not bandied about."

We were doing a lot of nodding around here this morning.

"The position is," he continued, "that my client has a daughter. She has regrettably fallen in with the —um—wrong people, and finally left home. We believe she may be here in Monkton City."

I took out a fresh note pad and pencil. It wasn't necessary, but I've learned that the customers like you to take notes.

"Why Monkton?" I asked.

Holford looked uncomfortable.

"The fact is," he said reluctantly, "the girl was not alone when she left."

"And the man is from around here?" I suggested.

"Well, one can't be positive, but certainly he has been known to boast of his business interests in this city."

"Do you know his name?"

He shrugged.

"I know what he called himself in Waldron. His real name could be anything."

It was very evident that Mr Holford didn't like any of this one little bit. Missing daughter, shady character, private eyes. This was not Mr Holford's pot of coffee. He wanted to get back to his real estate and lawsuits. And he wasn't exactly lavish with his information.

"Well, we have to start with something," I pointed out.

"Flegenheimer. Arthur Flegenheimer."

13

The pencil paused of its own volition. I felt a quiet despair, having dismissed a reaction that Holford was putting me on. He wasn't the kind. This was going to be a lulu.

"Mr Holford, I take your point. It seems very likely that you are correct in assuming this to be a false name."

His eyebrows lifted, possibly one twentieth of an inch.

"Why? True enough, it isn't a common name, but I've heard many stranger."

I laid the pencil down.

"Arthur, fine. Flegenheimer, fine. But Arthur Flegenheimer, both at the same time, that's too much. Forty years ago, in New York, there was a big racketeer called Dutch Schultz. You may have heard the name?"

He frowned, and thought for a moment.

"Yes, yes, I believe I have. But I don't—"

"That wasn't his real name."

I let it hang there till he grabbed at it.

"Oh dear. And this was?"

"It was. You see, if you told me a man by this name joined your country club, or went fishing with you, I wouldn't give it a second thought. But when you're telling me about a suspicious character who runs away with daughters as a side line, the coincidence is too much."

He inclined his head.

"Agreed, Mr Preston, I'm beginning to think I've come to the right man."

14

"A little early for that," I told him. "So we forget the name. How about this man's description?"

Manicured fingers drummed lightly on the desk top.

"About five feet ten inches. A little heavy, should we say perhaps one ninety to two hundred pounds. Age thirty to thirty-five. Dark hair. Nose rather prominent. Always well-dressed. In fact, rather over-dressed, if you follow me."

"H'm."

I was doing some quick calculations in my head. Even in Monkton the odds were not in my favour, but if I included the surrounding towns, not to mention the city of the Angels, I could come up with perhaps a hundred thousand guys who would fit Holford's picture.

"Nothing to narrow the field?" I asked without hope. "Maybe a wooden leg or a missing ear?"

He smiled thinly.

"I'm afraid not. I've never met the man myself, but I believe he does not even have a gold ring through his nose."

Jokes already. My smile was equally thin.

"No doubt we'll do better with the girl," I suggested.

He'd been waiting for it. Almost as I spoke, a photograph lay in front of me.

The picture was in colour. The naughty daughter was tallish, say five seven. The pieces of material which appeared here and there were no doubt supposed to represent a bathing suit. They certainly did nothing to disguise the fact that the wearer was one hundred per cent female, and beautiful with it. I looked at the honey blonde hair, and the grey eyes which seemed to be looking thoughtfully at something over my shoulder. Whoever Arthur Flegenheimer was, I could see his point of view.

"Beautiful," I conceded. "And her age?"

"Twenty-three. That's one of the problems, you see. The girl is of age. She can go where she pleases and with whom she pleases. Otherwise I should have gone to the police instead of coming here. No disrespect, you understand."

I understood.

"Tell me, does she have any money?"

"Oh, yes. She hasn't much by way of capital, but she has an annual income of fifty thousand. Of course, that is very little compared to her ultimate expectations."

"Mr Holford, I'm sure you will have thought of this before, but is there any way of stopping access to this income?"

"You are absolutely correct, and I have been in to the point most carefully. The answer is no. And the money is not even sent to her, so we can discount that avenue for tracing her address. Her cheques are acceptable anywhere in the U.S.A."

Great. I could probably trace this one in say two years or so, if the luck was running my way.

"Does she have any strong interests? I mean, is she a baseball buff, or a concert goer, or anything of that kind?"

"Not that I am aware of."

"One last thing. I'll have to know her name."

16

Those fingers went to work again.

"Very well. It's Carrington. Louise Carrington. And now I think you appreciate just how vital it is that this matter is handled with the utmost care."

Indeed I did. Edward F. Carrington was one of the leading political figures in the state. One of the very few politicians who'd never had any mud stick to him. I could imagine what the opposition press would make of his daughter's association with this Flegenheimer.

"Let's talk some more about the man." I leaned back. "Why are you so sure he's no good? I mean have you anything positive to go on?"

"Positive, no," he admitted. "But he lived in an expensive apartment, spent a great deal of money, always cash, and had no apparent form of occupation."

I didn't believe it myself, but the question had to be put.

"Family money, perhaps?"

I got that fleeting smile again.

"I'm afraid that Mr Flegenheimer's speech, his general manner, and his behaviour do not indicate an old New England background. No, he could be a gambler, or worse, but he has access to apparently unlimited funds."

"Plus a possible fifty thousand per," I added.

"That too," he agreed.

"These so-called business interests here, did he ever say what they were, and what they connected with?"

He shook his head firmly.

"Not so far as I have been able to ascertain. But

17

then, if they are, as I suspect, on the doubtful side of the law, that ought to restrict your field of inquiry, I imagine."

"Agreed." I stared out of the window before asking my next question.

"About Miss Carrington. What sort of a girl is she? Is she normally the quiet type, or what?"

"I wouldn't call Louise quiet, by any means. She's always had plenty of friends, a busy social life. A bit headstrong, wilful if you like. But considering her wealthy background, and her upbringing, she's a very sensible person. Many young people in her position develop some rather undesirable characteristics, such as believing that the world was only created for their personal benefit. She is not like that."

Whatever she was like, she certainly had one friend, I mused.

"Mr Holford, if I find her, and I emphasise the if, what do you want me to do?"

"I'll have to rely on your judgement, to some extent. If the circumstances are such that you think you can persuade her to go home, then do so. If you think you can buy this man off, contact me and we'll discuss the terms."

I held up a finger.

"I've seen that one bounce. The man takes the money, and then the girl won't leave him. Or, he leaves town, and the girl still refuses to go home. Your client could find himself a good deal out of pocket, and still not get his daughter back. That won't do him any good, and it won't help my reputation."

His eyes gleamed appreciatively.

18

"That is good thinking, Mr Preston. However, I fall back on my legal training. It is always unwise to prejudge the outcome of any issue until the issue itself is clearly defined. Or, in more simple terms, don't let's cross our bridges until we come to them. The first thing is to find the girl. That will probably be the most difficult part."

I could go along with him there.

"And now, there is the question of your fees."

I told him my prices, and he didn't seem surprised.

"That is acceptable. My client will retain you for five days, after which we shall discuss your progress, and whether there is any point in continuing. If you find the girl, there will be a bonus of five hundred dollars. If, as a result of your efforts, she goes back to her father, there will be a further bonus of one thousand dollars. Is that satisfactory?"

"I would say it's generous," I conceded. "Do I call you at this number?"

I tapped at his card.

"Between 9 a.m. and 6, yes. Otherwise, this is my house number."

He scribbled with a gold pencil. I edged my wooden one respectfully to one side.

"We have an agreement then, Mr Preston."

He stood up and held out his hand.

"In addition to being my client, Ed Carrington is one of my closest friends," he said quietly. "I know what this is doing to him, so it's more than mere business that makes me wish you good luck."

"I'll try."

19

His back was very straight as he went out. I flicked at the buzzer.

"Miss Digby, will you come in?"

Florence Digby appeared, cool and remote as always, in a yellow two-piece suit.

"We have a client," I handed over the card. "When you've made a note, let me have it back, please. I may need to call him out of hours. Start booking my time and expenses as of now. This is the one about the missing daughter."

She sniffed.

"Funny how it's always the daughter. Why doesn't anyone want you to find the missing son?"

I grinned.

"Maybe all those cases go to female private detectives."

She put the card back on the table and went out. I walked over to the window and leaned against it. Somewhere out there was a girl named Louise Carrington, who could be worth a lot of money to me. Not to mention a joker named Arthur Flegenheimer. He'd probably changed that by now. I ought to ask around for somebody called Capone or Dillinger or you name it. Well, I wasn't going to find anybody staring out of windows. I took out the phone book, sat down and began to dial.

2

Two hours, and twenty plus telephone calls later, I leaned back and took another Old Favorite from the rapidly emptying pack. I could have sworn Louise Carrington's expression had acquired just a touch of mockery as she stared up at me from the desk.

Miss Digby buzzed me.

"Sam Thompson is here."

"Send him in."

Sam is probably the laziest man in the U.S. of A. Certainly no one in Monkton could come within a mile of him. But he has this problem everyone has. He has to eat, and he has to pay his rent. So he does a little of this and a little of that to cover expenses. He also has somewhat of a thirst. One of the things he does best, when he's hungry or thirsty enough, is to work for me as a leg-man. And he's very good at it.

SOMEBODY HAS TO LOSE

He shambled in, the unhappy face watchful as ever, and parked himself in the visitor's chair.

" 'Lo Preston. I hear you've been looking for me."

"Right."

I pushed across a cigaret, moving the pack out of reach of his hand just in time. Then I slid Louise Carrington's picture under his nose.

"I want to find this girl."

He stared at her and shrugged.

"Who doesn't?"

I told him some of the story, just the parts he needed to know.

"Does she have a name?"

"She does, but she won't be using it. The first name's Louise, but I can't even guarantee she'll use that."

"Is there a picture of the guy?"

"No. And not much of a description either."

I told him how Holford had described Mr Flegen-heimer. He liked the bit about the name.

"I could ask around," he suggested. "Find out if there's any new talent in town."

"Me too. And also if anyone has been out of the city for a couple of months. Don't forget, this character claimed he already had interests around here."

"Right. Er—about my expenses. Does Daddy run to those?"

"He runs to expenses incurred on the job," I told him. "Not to you sitting around in some bar for three days straight."

He looked pained.

22

"Trouble with you, Preston, this job makes you cynical. Cynical and world-weary."

"Just keep the expenses down, and show how wrong I am."

He made to put the photograph in his pocket.

"Sorry, that's the only one I have."

He took a reluctant last look at her, and passed the picture back.

"If I find her, what do I do?"

"Nothing. Just call me."

He stood up.

"I could use a little car-fare."

I handed him two tens.

"We don't have a lot of time. Just three days, so keep at it."

After he'd gone, I checked my watch. It was three in the afternoon, and I wondered fleetingly whether Louise might have decided to go horseracing. One thing was certain, she was not going to come knocking on my door. I put the picture in my billfold and went out. Florence Digby looked up.

"If Sam calls here while I'm not around, don't let him have more than twenty dollars at one time."

"Right. Where can I reach you?"

"I wish I knew," I told her. "She could be anywhere. I'll try to look in some time tomorrow."

Down the street, a man just avoided bumping into me. He was about thirty, had dark hair and was overweight. I avoided the temptation to ask him if he'd run away with any daughters lately.

*   *   *

23

By seven thirty in the evening, I had made a lot of no progress, and was getting weary. My suit was looking crumpled, and I thought it was time to get home and freshen up. It could be a long night.

Home is an expensive apartment at Parkside Towers. The way I see it, a man likely to collect as many bruises as I do, is entitled to nurse them in comfort. I put on some coffee, and while it was brewing, stripped off my clothes and stepped under the shower. The needle spray soothed away the weariness, and ten minutes later I was seated watching television with coffee and Old Favorites to hand. It was the Brick Radford series, which fascinates me. This week, he has to find half-a-million dollars and the time-slot allowed him fifty-one minutes in which to do it. I wasn't concerned. Old Brick would come through. Only the week before he had personally bumped off four Chinese thugs who'd kidnapped a baby. Finding a few treasury bills would be a cinch. When I get in a fight, my face gets bloodied up, shirt torn, and I look like something that fell in a meat mincer. Not Brick. He always comes up looking like an ad for shaving cream. Right on time he produced the money, narrowly missing death twice, and drove off my screen with a stacked blonde. Blonde. Louise was blonde. Maybe if I contacted Brick, and offered to split my fee, he would find her for me. Within the stipulated fifty-one minutes, naturally. Silly idea. He had his own blonde, and why would he work for my kind of money? I switched off, swallowed the last of the coffee, and dressed. It was nine o'clock

24

when I closed the door behind me, and went out into the darkening city.

Although the sky knew it was late, the concrete thought it was still noon, and the heat bounced at me from every side as I rolled the Chev into the heart of the city. I parked the car a few yards away from my destination and climbed out. The neon sign was discreet, by Monkton standards. The place is called the Oyster's Cloister, and it's run by a friend of mine, Reuben Krantz.

The doorman looked unhappy in his blue uniform.

" 'Lo, Biff," I greeted.

"Hey, Mr Preston. Long time no see. Little hot for eating, ain't it?"

"Too hot," I agreed. "It's always too hot at these prices. Boss in?"

"It's after nine. You can bet he is."

I went into the welcome cool of the lobby, and tapped at a door marked "Private". Krantz was sitting behind his huge desk, hands clasped in front of him, listening intently to the radio. He waved me to a chair, and I sat down. The fights were on tonight in L.A. and he was listening to the commentary on the preliminaries. A roar went up from the crowd, and he switched off abruptly.

"Fifty bucks," he said sadly. "These cream puffs today, I don't know why I bother."

"Some boy you're interested in?" I queried.

"I have twenty-five per cent of him. The Lord alone knows why. I could probably take him myself."

He probably could, at that. At fifty, he was still in good trim. Dark, powerfully built, he was very much

25

the same man he'd been years before, and he wasn't running any restaurant in those days. The Oyster's Cloister was the best for miles around, but some of the clientele would have raised an eyebrow if they knew the history of their distinguished host. But he'd left all that behind him now, and spent most of his time and money chasing the elusive remedy for some obscure stomach complaint he had.

He made a note on his desk-pad and looked up.

"You want something," he stated. "I never see you any other time."

"That's what friends are for," I reminded. "I'm looking for a girl."

"What kind of girl? Anyway, I don't traffic in girls."

I took out Louise's picture and lay it in front of him.

"This girl everybody's looking for," he said appreciatively. "What did she do?"

"Nothing. She just left home and her white-haired old Daddy wants her back."

He nodded.

"I haven't got her. If I had, I wouldn't be sitting here chewing the fat with you."

I broke out my Old Favorites, and pushed one into my face.

"There's a man involved," I told him.

"So?"

"This guy seems to be mixed up in some kind of racket here in Monkton. He's been out of town a few weeks, and I wondered if you might know of somebody who's been missing."

He squinted suspiciously.

"Why would I know about people like that? For that matter, what's this character done that's so terrible? This one," he tapped at the photograph, "is of age. Or is this the story about the white slave traffic?"

"No. As for the man, you're probably right. What I hear of this girl, when she's ready she'll leave him."

"So?"

He waved his arms expressively. I slipped a low punch.

"But that doesn't help her father. She's all he has."

Krantz has three daughters, whom he worships. He frowned, scratched irritably at his wrist.

"H'm. You want some beer?"

The question, as they say, was rhetorical. He stood up, slid back a mahogany book-case, and dived behind it. When he reappeared, he carried two tall glasses of ice-cold beer. It tasted good.

"I was always taught to mind my own business," he grumbled. "I don't like meddling in people's affairs. This guy, what does he look like?"

I gave him the only description I had. He snorted.

"That's easy. I got four, maybe five guys like that eating their heads off outside right now. Take any one you want. Does he have a name?"

That got me a laugh, at least.

"I'm beginning to like the guy," he chuckled. "He marches into a strange town, takes off with a dame who looks like this, and has class with it. And as for that name."

He laughed again.

"Preston, I'm glad you dropped in. People should keep in touch. But I have some folks waiting for me, so I got to give you the rush."

I was disappointed. He either couldn't or wouldn't help me. I drained the last of the beer and got up.

"Good beer," I acknowledged. "I'll see you, Ben."

As I opened the door, he called after me.

"You seen Mournful lately? He hasn't given me a bad tip in weeks."

"No, I haven't."

"Well, if you run into him, give him my regards."

"Right."

I was thoughtful as I climbed back into the car. Mournful Harris is a guy who specialises in handing out information, mostly bad, about racehorses. The sucker bets so much, and Mourful gets a piece of the action if it comes good. Or he will sell the information outright. I had a good idea where he'd be found at that hour, and I pointed the Chev downtown.

Benito's is a pool-hall. At least, that's what the sign says. He really does have a couple of tables up there, and I've even seen guys playing on them from time to time. But it's really a kind of club. For horse-players. They sit around on the wooden benches that line the walls, arguing interminably about the reasons why they hadn't cleaned up on the day's racing. To them, the whole racing world was a set-up. Every owner, trainer and jockey was a crook. Every stable boy had his pockets stuffed with goof balls. Even track officials were on the make. Horses were temperamental, unreliable, lazy. At least, that was how things stood up to and including today. Tomorrow was

28

going to be very different. Tomorrow's horses were being run by honest men, who really knew the sport. The horses too, were triers, who would be running their hearts out for the financial benefit of Benito's customers. You wouldn't find them present tomorrow night, no sir. They'd be throwing a big party at the L.A. Hilton, or maybe on the night flight to Bermuda. Nobody paid me any attention as I entered the steamy, smoke-filled hall. Most of them knew me by sight, and although I didn't have the bug, at least I made a bet occasionally.

The man I wanted was leaning against the far wall, in deep conversation with a fat man who was, for some reason, wearing a pink jockey's cap.

"Hi, Mournful."

He turned his unhappy face maybe one quarter inch in my direction.

"Mr Preston, glad to see you."

A stranger would never have known it. The long thin face, with the drooping jowls, had the expression of a man who'd just lost his best friend.

"You got a minute?"

It was a gag really. Mournful always has a minute. In fact, lots of minutes. The man in the pink cap did a fade.

"Didn't mean to interrupt your friend," I apologised.

"Friend?" The sad eyes rolled. "You know what Fattie was trying to do? He only tried to sell me information, is all. A personal friend of every trainer in the country. And most of the nags too."

I looked at the threadbare suit and greasy shirt.

"Must be a stranger," I suggested. "Everybody knows you're well connected, Mournful."

"That's right," he agreed. "Well, how you been, Mr Preston?"

I told him how I'd been, and how'd he been, and it seemed he'd been fine up until today, when some crooked jock put the brakes on, a half-furlong from home. Luckily, and he was willing to share his luck with me, he had inside information on a fixed race out at Palmtrees which was taking place tomorrow.

"You ought to clean up," I told him. "Let's sit down a minute."

We parked on one of the hard benches, well out of earshot of the other people present.

"I might be able to stake you to a little capital."

This is always a good opener with Mournful. Or any other horseplayer. Capital is all they need. Just those initial few dollars which will be the first stepping stone on the road to tens of thousands. A quick look round the room did not produce anybody who seemed to be in that bracket, but as I reminded myself, that was because they, the big winners, were out throwing parties. Or on the night flight to Bermuda.

The bloodhound eyes gleamed briefly.

"Who do I have to kill?"

"Nobody. I'm just looking for some people."

I told him about Flegenheimer, leaving out the name.

"Could be anybody," he shrugged. "The tracks are full of guys who look like that."

"This one's a spender," I persisted. "He is also

30

either a new man, or a regular who's been out of town for a few weeks."

In the effort of concentration, he actually contrived to add a further furrow to the army of lines on his forehead.

"Nothing happens," he admitted ruefully. "And I sure could use a little of that capital."

I'd been saving the girl. Ben Krantz hadn't sent me here for no reason.

"There's also a girl."

I showed him the picture and he stared. Girls are not one of Mournful's strong points. If she'd had four legs and a tail, he'd have placed her within seconds. He held her at arm's length, squinting.

After several seconds, he sighed.

"This one, I've seen."

I managed to keep the smirk off my face and waited.

"I've seen this one. And lately."

The mental effort was putting a strain on him. I would have to be patient, while his mind tried to dissociate itself from important matters, and think for a while about people. Especially girl people. The Old Favorite added its two cents worth to the general fug.

"At the track. Two, maybe three days ago."

"Why do you remember her? She's just another dame, and there must have been thousands there."

"Ordinarily, yes. But there was some kind of trouble."

I tucked Louise back in my pocket.

"Trouble?" I prompted.

"Yeah. I didn't see it personally. These two guys

31

got in a fight. Nothing to it really. Just two punches, I was told. Somebody broke it up before I got close, but that one," he pointed to my pocket, "was with one of them."

I sat quietly, hoping for more. Then he came as close to smiling as I've seen him.

"And now it comes back, the guy she was with could be this big spender we've been talking about. Could just be."

"Does he have a name?"

"Probably. But I wouldn't know it."

He wasn't holding out. He could smell money, and would tell me anything he knew to translate that smell into feel.

"What was the fight about?"

"I don't know that either."

It began to look like a blind alley, but I wasn't going to give up. Krantz had as good as told me to find Harris. He could probably have made life a lot easier by telling me himself what I wanted to know, but that wasn't his style. The way he looked at the world, I was getting paid to find things out, and I'd better get out there and find them. He wouldn't mind shortening the price by dropping Mournful Harris' name, but after that I was on my own.

"Do you know the guy he slugged?"

"Him? I would hope so. It was Laramie."

The world looked good again. I knew Laramie James, and he was at least on punching terms with my man. The way I see it, you have to have a reason for slugging people, and that implies at least some personal acquaintance, however slight.

32

"And that's all you can tell me?"

"That's it, Mr Preston. Honest, if I knew—"

"I know," I cut in. "What about this red-hot information you have?"

"Fourth race, tomorrow," he pronounced positively. "Naughty Woman, a ten to one shot."

I swear Louise wriggled in my pocket.

"I'll put ten on her nose," I promised. "You get twenty-five per cent."

He looked even more morose.

"I kind of like to make my own wagers."

"O.K."

I gave him five and left.

3

Two hours and about seven bars later, I stared sadly at the mug of suds in front of me. There was probably some beer in there some place, if a man had the time and patience to search for it, but mostly it was suds. As a TV commercial for detergent, it would have been a knockout. The place was called Soapy Sam's or maybe Steamy Sid's, I wouldn't remember. After two hours they all look alike. I'd stared into a lot of suds, and yacked it up with a lot of Sids and Sams, but I hadn't come up with Laramie James.

James is strictly small time. He does whatever comes along to hustle a buck, and isn't too particular about the details. The law never had anything powerful enough to tie him in, but they were always interested in his little goings on. An elbow dug into my ribs, and he was sitting on the next stool.

"Hear you're looking for me."

He was tallish with bright red hair, and although I hadn't seen him arrive, I knew his loping, bandy style of walking that had earned him his cowboy nickname.

"Right," I confirmed. "What'll you drink?"

He looked at the detergent and shrugged.

"Rye."

I ordered and he picked up the glass.

"Mud," he saluted. "So what can I do for you?"

"I hear you got in a fight out at the track."

I made it a question. He nodded, grinning.

"Not much of a fight, though. One punch apiece, and then people stopped all the fun. What about it? Does the guy want to sue me?"

"I wouldn't know," I replied. "I don't even know who he was."

"Then why all the interest?" he queried.

"There's something I'm working on. From what I hear of the man you had the fight with, I think he may be able to help me."

His eyes brightened, and then grew narrow.

"Sounds like this might be a reward situation. Is that right? I mean there's maybe a piece of change in this for old Laramie?"

"Only a small piece," I advised him. "I don't know who he is yet, and even when I find out, I can't be sure it's the right guy."

"H'm." He considered this. "How small?"

"Five."

The red hair wagged from side to side.

"Let's make it ten."

35

"All right. But that's tops. Do you know his name?"

"Well, I didn't when we had our little chat, but somebody told me later. He's Barney Stillman."

The name stirred a faint chord.

"Stillman," I repeated. "I've heard it some place."

"Right. He's part owner of a joint out on 66. The Green Parrot."

That was it. I remembered now. There'd been some trouble out there a while back, although the details escaped me.

"What did you fight about?" I wanted to know.

"There was this broad with him," he explained. "Stillman said I pinched her ass."

"And did you?"

He grinned.

"Just a little bit."

I almost reached for Louise's picture, but changed my mind. If Laramie was certain I was on the right track, he was quite capable of going either to Stillman or the girl. In exchange for another ten, he would impart the good news that a private eye had been asking questions about them. They could decide to go to ground.

"Preston, since I'm drinking your rye, I'll give you some free advice. This guy is bad news. If I knew then what I know now, I'd have kept my hands in my pockets."

"Well, thanks, Laramie, but he's not my man. The guy I want is strictly on the legit, so I can cross your candidate off."

36

He looked disappointed.

"Something was said about ten?"

"Sure," I handed him the bill. "Even eliminating people is still worth something."

"Thanks." The note disappeared from view. "Sorry it wasn't any good. Hope you find him."

And he was gone. I sat there for another ten minutes to give him time to get well clear of the place. Then I pushed the suds back towards the bar jockey.

"I already have a clean shirt," I explained.

He said something my old maiden aunt would not have understood as I made for the door.

*   *   *

The Green Parrot is not to be confused with Soapy Sam's. It lies back from the highway about one quarter mile, and you can tell right away that to go inside is going to cost money. I drove into the enormous car park, avoiding the cheaper models, and finally selected a spot next to a gleaming Alfa-Romeo and within nodding distance of a Rolls-Royce.

My feet scrunched on the gravel as I made for the well-lit entrance.

Inside, the evening was in full swing. There were three bars, and a restaurant where you could dance. A small group was playing some effective Cole Porter and I leaned in the doorway listening to them for a few minutes. The drummer looked up, saw me, and waved one of his sticks. That's the story of my life. Here I was, surrounded by people with all kinds of money, but the only one in the joint who knew me was the drummer. I waved back, and wandered into the nearest bar.

It was cool and quiet in there. It was also badly lit, the kind of place where you could buy your best friend's wife a quiet drink without much fear of being seen.

The crimson-coated jockey was a good-looking negro, busily polishing at a glass with an immaculate white cloth.

"What can I get you, sir?"

I ordered scotch on the rocks, and admired the professional performance which went into its preparation. To most people it's a simple matter of dropping some ice into a glass and slopping scotch over the top. This guy made the whole thing into a kind of ritual, as though the secret had been handed down by his dear old father. When I looked at how much change I received from a five dollar bill, I decided that the ritual qualified for some kind of entertainment tax.

He watched anxiously as I took my first sip.

"Fine," I said.

He was relieved, smiling quickly and getting busy again with his cloth.

"Mr Stillman here tonight?" I asked.

The cloth stopped moving for a moment, then resumed its brisk rubbing.

"I don't know, sir. He doesn't always come. Anything I can do for you?"

"Nope. Want to see him personally."

He must have given some kind of signal, though I didn't spot it. A man appeared beside me. He was

38

young, handsome in an aggressive kind of way. The voice was that of a man who'd been to school.

"Can I help you, sir?"

'Maybe. Are you Stillman?"

I knew he wasn't. The reason for asking the question was to let him know that I was not acquainted with the man I was asking for.

He shook his head.

"No. Just a humble employee. What did you want to see him about?"

"Sorry, this is private business."

He eyed me carefully. He'd know me again.

"Please wait here. I'll see if Mr Stillman is in the club."

He was back before I'd had time to finish my drink.

"Will you come with me?"

I followed him through some black velvet curtains that hid a small corridor. My guide walked to the door at the end and knocked. There was a voice from inside and I was motioned in.

A man sat behind a desk, a man who fitted the description I'd been given.

"I'm Stillman," he announced. "Who're you?"

"The name is Preston."

"So what can I do for you?"

I looked at my guide, or more probably, guard.

"It's kind of private."

He looked thoughtful.

"Wait outside, Roy."

Roy didn't move.

"He has a gun," he announced.

Stillman chuckled.

"Roy is very observant. Also, he worries about my health. That's what I pay him for. Is that right about the gun?"

I nodded.

"Sure. But that's got nothing to do with why I'm here."

"Maybe. Maybe not." He brought up his hand from behind the desk. He was holding a .32 revolver. "You see, I worry about my health too. Why don't you just put your gun down someplace out of reach, and we can have our little chat."

The .32 was unwavering as I took out my Police Special and put it on a chair.

"Roy."

Roy picked it up and shot out the clip, which he placed in his pocket.

"You get it back when you leave," my host assured me.

He nodded to the observant Roy, who went quietly out.

Stillman relaxed back in his chair.

"Now, what's all this private business?"

I showed him my buzzer. He looked amused.

"A private badge. So?"

"There's a girl missing," I told him.

"There always is," he returned. "And?"

"And I think you may be able to help me find her."

He laughed. He probably did it to show off his good teeth.

"Keep talking," he invited. "There has to be more."

Well, at least I hadn't been thrown out. Not yet.

"This girl is over twenty-one. That means she can go where she choses. Within the limits of the law, she can also do as she likes. She has family. They want me to find her."

"And you?" he questioned. "What do you want?"

I gazed at him evenly.

"I want to talk to her. If she left home of her own free will, and is not being held against that will, if she's safe and in good health, then there's nothing I or anybody else can do about her. Like I said, she's over twenty-one."

He nodded, making unnecessary smoothing motions at his immaculate lapel.

"I always heard you had a helluva nerve. People were right. This girl now, what's her name?"

"Louise Carrington."

I watched him as I said it, but his eyes didn't waver.

"I was starting to think it might be. Give me a reason why I don't have you bounced around a little and heaved o t on your fanny."

I sighed.

"The first reason is I already collected enough lumps in this bad old world."

He grinned quickly.

"No good. You got a second reason?"

"The second reason is, you got more brains. You throw me out, O.K. I put a couple of guys on your tail, sooner or later they locate the girl anyway. It could take days, cost a lot of money. It's foolish. There's no need to turn a two-reeler into a million dollar wide-screen production. That is, always assuming the girl is here of her own choice. If she is, what are we fighting about?"

He sat and thought about it.

"Makes sense," he decided. "You know Louise?"

"No, never met her."

He chuckled.

"I thought not. Anybody thinks he can keep that one, when she doesn't want to be kept, needs his brains scrambled. I'll have to tell her what you said. O.K., you can see her."

"And no lumps."

"Not if you behave."

He looked at his watch.

"She'll be here in about thirty minutes. Why don't you park it outside, and have a drink or two. When Louise arrives, I'll let you know."

"I want to see her alone," I told him.

"Why?"

"She may be afraid of you for all I know."

He tilted back his head and guffawed.

"Louise?" he said incredulously. "It's a sure thing you don't know her. I'd as soon pick a fight with a grizzly bear. Afraid of me."

He laughed again.

"About the gun," I interrupted.

"Sure, take it, take it. But we'll just leave it empty for a while. And by the way, around here she's Miss Russel."

I went back to the bar, where the sounds of music

42

filtered quietly through, and sat nursing a tall cold glass. Roy looked in at me from time to time, just to ensure I wasn't robbing the till. People drifted in and out, quiet twosomes, noisy groups, an occasional loner. Three-quarters of an hour went by. Louise, it would appear, was not a good time-keeper.

I didn't see her arrive. I was staring at the wall, when Stillman's voice said, "Well, you wanted to meet the lady."

I looked around, and stood up fast. She was a knockout, far more so even than the photograph had suggested. The cream dress left plenty of spaces for the golden-brown flesh to show through.

"How do you do, Miss Russel," I mumbled.

"I'm fine."

She flashed a brilliant smile, and I decided I could learn to hate Barney Stillman.

"Buy the lady a drink," he invited. "I'll be back in a few minutes."

She looked at me impishly.

"I'd like some Campari and soda."

While I was getting it, she went across to sit at one of the low tables round the wall. Every man in the place watched her.

I went over with the drinks and sat next to her.

"M'm, this is nice. Could I have a cigaret?"

She could have a cigaret. She could have the whole pack, plus anything else I possessed that might give her any pleasure. Not excluding me.

"You're making me uneasy," she said without conviction. "Looking at me that way. I feel you might try to eat me at any minute."

"Will there be an opportunity?"

She chuckled.

"You're a funny sort of detective. I thought you were supposed to wear shabby suits, and spy on bed-rooms."

"Only the second-class variety. The good ones, like me, sit around in expensive bars with expensive women. Anyway, I don't like shabby suits."

"I can see that. Let's get down to brass tacks, Mr Preston. All right, you found me. What is supposed to happen next?"

I set my glass down on the table.

"Probably nothing, as far as I am concerned. I am to find you, satisfy myself that you are alive and well—"

"—Yes to both—" she butted in.

"—and also that you are not being held here under any kind of restraint."

She held out the slim brown hands.

"See? No handcuffs."

I nodded.

"Agreed. But there are other forms of restraints."

She looked puzzled.

"For example?"

"For example there's fear. You could be afraid of this man."

Louise chuckled again.

"I've never been afraid of any man in my life. Cross that one off."

"And there's blackmail."

I watched her face closely, but the reaction was nil.

44

"Sorry. Nobody's holding any letters tied in red ribbon. Nobody saw me leave the scene of the crime. I'm here because I choose to be. Satisfied?"

"Yes, I think I am."

Satisfied, and disappointed, both at the same time. I didn't care for the idea of her choosing to be with Stillman.

"What will you do now, Mr Preston?"

"I'll report that I found you, and we had this conversation. And I'll say where you can be located."

"But you don't know my address," she objected.

I looked pained.

"Oh, come on, Miss Russel. You're not going to make me follow you home, or some such foolishness, surely?"

She hesitated.

"Well, I suppose it would be rather childish. O.K. 702, Cheviot Apartments. It's on Hillside Drive."

I scribbled it down.

"Telephone?"

"What do you need that for?"

"Purely personal. You might feel like dinner some evening."

She shook her head in wonder.

"You really are the oddest detective. I believe I'm going to tell you."

And she did.

"You haven't asked me why I left home."

I shrugged.

"A, it's none of my business, and B, I would imagine it's because of Stillman."

"Barney? Oh, he's all right, but this is no white-hot burning romance thing. No, I've been intending to leave Waldron for a long time. Barney just provided the extra incentive."

She paused, as if deciding whether to tell me more. And decided against it.

"What's your first name?" she asked instead.

"Mark. Why?"

"When people buy me drinks and offer me dinner, I at least expect to know their names. Mark Preston. I like it."

Suddenly, I liked it too. She stood up.

"I have to go. Perhaps we'll meet again."

"I certainly hope so."

There was hush in the bar as she walked away and out of view. I looked up to find that Roy was standing in front of me.

"Mr Stillman says goodnight," he told me flatly. "He also says goodbye."

Evidently, if I was going to be buying any dinners, it was not to be at the Green Parrot.

"O.K. I was leaving anyway."

Outside, the air was pleasantly cool now. On the drive back to town I found myself humming some old Maurice Chevalier number.

What was it again?

Oh, yes.

Louise.

4

I CALLED Holford the next morning.

"Who wants him, please?"

"The name is Preston. From Monkton City."

Some clicking, and I heard a woman's voice.

"Good morning, Mr Preston. I am Mrs Stevens, Mr Holford's personal secretary. What can I do for you?"

"It's a private matter," I told her.

She wasn't impressed.

"I handle all Mr Holford's affairs, Mr Preston. Most of our business is highly confidential. You may speak to me quite freely."

"Not about this," I contradicted. "Mr Holford can confide in you if he wants, but not me."

The voice at the other end dropped temperature several degrees.

"I am afraid Mr Holford is extremely busy. He does not take direct calls without my personal clearance."

"Mrs Stevens," I said wearily, "I don't know whether you're being efficient or just plain nosey, but I have to speak to Mr Holford personally. And he won't be very pleased with you if I don't get through."

She thought about it.

"From Monkton City, you said?"

"That's what I said."

"Hold the line please."

I held the line, not too patiently. More clicking, and a man said, "Mr Preston? Good morning."

"Mr Holford, I have some news for you."

"Ah. Not on this line, if you please. Are you in your office?"

"Yes."

"I will call you back directly."

And I was tolding a dead phone. So much for Mrs Personal Clearance Stevens.

He was back within minutes.

"This is a clear line, Mr Preston. What have you learned?"

"I found her."

"Good heavens. So quickly?"

"It was just luck, Mr Holford. I've talked with her, and I'm satisfied she's a free agent. I have her address, if you want to make a note."

I had a mental picture of the slim gold pencil working as I told him where Louise was.

"And the man Flegenheimer?" he queried.

48

"His real name is Stillman. Barney Stillman. He's either the owner, or at least part-owner of a place called the Green Parrot. It's an expensive club, from which I am barred, effective last evening."

He gave a dry laugh.

"You seem to have been very busy. How was Louise?"

"Calm, self-assured, not in the least worried about anything, so far as I could judge. What do you want me to do now, Mr Holford?"

"Nothing. I must get in touch with her father. If there is anything further I shall contact you. You really have done excellently, Mr Preston. I shall send your fee at once. And thank you."

"Thank you, Mr Holford."

And we hung up.

For no good reason, I thought of Mournful Harris. What was the name of that horse he gave me? I took the *Herald* out of the waste basket and ran my eyes down the runners. There she was. Naughty Woman.

The last three pieces of hot information I'd had from Mournful had all turned sour. By the law of averages, he had to be right some time.

I phoned Keppler and put fifty on the nose.

"Naughty Woman?" he chuckled. "That's the quickest fifty bucks I'll make today. Do you realise, Preston, that nag is so old she was a personal friend of Sea Biscuit?"

"But I have this red-hot information," I assured him.

"I hope you get plenty more like it," he replied. "I could retire in a year. Fifty it is."

After which encouraging chat I went home.

I took a shower and paddled around, with a can of ice cold beer. Having picked up some book twice and found I couldn't concentrate, I finally came up with the afternoon movie. A gripping drama, I was assured. It gripped me so hard, I was asleep in ten minutes.

Something woke me. The gripping drama was over, and a man with very long and seemingly dirty hair, was explaining how I should cook my roast beef, English-style.

What woke me was the telephone.

"Preston?"

It sounded like Keppler.

"Yeah," I admitted.

"Where'd you get your red-hot information?" he demanded. "That lump of catsmeat just passed the post at twelve to one. I'm in to you for six hundred bucks."

The world looked good again.

"I guess I should have told you before. The horse is a relative. But I thought it was ten to one?"

"Whaddya think, I'm maybe Santa Claus? The odds went up."

"Great. I'll see you tonight."

The temptation to call Louise Carrington was strong, but I decided it was too soon. Instead I went out on the town.

*   *   *

Two days later I was sitting in the office reading a stolen paintings bulletin when the buzzer went.

50

"Lieutenant Rourke is here."

"Have him come in."

The grizzled Irishman entered the room, Gil Randall close behind him.

"Hallo John, have a chair."

"Mark."

We looked at each other casually while they scraped chairs around. These two were probably the most formidable Homicide combination in the state. Rourke was tough, intelligent, indefatigable. And you couldn't buy him. Randall was big and slow moving. He didn't look all that bright, but he had a mind like a razor, and the slow frame could pounce like a tiger cat when occasion demanded. We'd all known each other a long time and had developed some kind of an understanding. Rourke knew I was more or less honest, even if some of my methods were devious.

"How's that slaughterhouse deal coming?" I asked conversationally.

There'd been a murder a month or so back, a real beauty if the newspapers were to be believed. A woman's body had been so badly cut about that the police wouldn't release even one picture for the newspapers, which is most unusual.

Rourke groaned.

"What do you want to bring that thing up for?"

"Nothing, huh? It sounded to me very similar to that Hollings Street job about a year ago."

"It looked a lot like it too," Randall told me. "Unless we have two gibbering maniacs in this city, it looks like the same guy."

"Why the interest?" Rourke wanted to know. He

51

fished out one of his evil little Spanish cigars and set about polluting the atmosphere.

I shrugged.

"Just natural. If I came up with anything on a case like that, everybody would love me. The public, the newspapers, even you two."

The Lieutenant looked at Randall, who said, "It can't do any harm. We know almost nothing anyway. And the way this character goes around sticking his nose into everybody else's business, you can never tell."

I watched the foul yellow smoke hanging in the air above the Irishman's head.

"Most of it was in the papers. Her name was Elaine Evans, twenty-six years old. She was a small-time actress, TV and radio mostly. She worked pretty often, had a good address, eight thousand dollars in stocks."

"Married?"

"Divorced. The husband left town two years ago. He's in Detroit. There were men around, but nobody special. By today's standards her morals were not all that bad."

"And the guy who did it?"

"Almost nothing. He left part of a footprint in the blood on the carpet, so we know what size shoes he wore. The depth of the indentation suggests medium height or over, weight one seventy or thereabouts."

"H'm."

When they said they had practically nothing, they meant it.

"Well, if that's all you have, with all your resources,

I'd better forget about it. Anyway, you didn't come here to talk about that."

"No." Rourke puffed furiously. "You know a guy named Barney Stillman?"

My little warning bell began to ring.

"I've met him."

"When?"

"Two, three nights ago. I was out at his place, the Green Parrot."

"That night, you had a fight with him?"

This from Randall.

"Fight? No. What would we fight about?"

"Tell him the joke, Sergeant."

Randall grinned.

"We ask the questions."

"Not here you don't," I said irritably. "You guys march in here, all chummy, suddenly it's an interrogation. If Stillman says we had a fight, he's a liar. And I'll say so to his face, with both of you present."

Rourke nodded solemnly.

"We could arrange that, of course. But it wouldn't carry any weight."

"It would prove he's lying."

The Lieutenant removed the chewed remnants of the weed from his mouth. Gratefully, I watched him crush it in the ashtray.

"Wouldn't prove a thing," he countered. "We have Stillman locked away. He hasn't any clothes on. What he does have is a label tied to one of his big toes, and three bullet holes in his chest."

So that was it.

"This is a murder enquiry. Don't obstruct us. What was the fight about?"

"There wasn't any fight," I repeated wearily. "We disagreed about something, he barred me from the club. That's all there was to it."

We all looked at each other.

"We're waiting for the rest," explained Randall.

"There was a girl. Stillman thought I was too interested in her."

"That sounds just enough like you to be the truth," observed Rourke.

"Who was the girl?"

"Louise something or other."

"And she was at the club that night?"

"Why, yes." My surprise was obvious. "How else could I pay her attention?"

Randall leaned forward.

"You could have known her weeks, months," he pointed out.

"That I would have liked. No, I just saw her that one time."

"And you don't know where she is now."

Rourke made it a statement.

"Right."

The two officers exchanged glances.

"You have a license for one .38 Police Special," stated Randall. "Is it around?"

"Sure."

I pulled open a drawer, and slid the cold metal across the desk. Rourke picked it up, sniffed, peeked inside. In a pained voice, he said, "Preston, this weapon is dirty. If you were one of my officers, this would cost you a week's pay."

"I'll clean it up," I promised.

He pushed it back.

"Just for the record, where were you between ten o'clock and midnight last night?"

That was easy.

"If I'm supposed to say I went to the movies and slept all through the programme, you're out of luck. I was out at Monkton High, listening to Oscar Peterson."

"Anybody see you?"

I chuckled.

"Let's start with Chief Humphries. He was two seats away. Then there was Larsen, covering the concert for the *Globe*. I had a talk with—"

He waved me down.

"O.K., O.K. It was just for the record. We're not very interested in you anyway. The one we want is the girl. But then, you don't know where she is."

"Sorry."

I helped myself to an Old Favorite. The fumes fought without hope against the Rourke butt.

"This girl," I said hesitantly, "she didn't impress me as the type to pump a man full of holes."

Both men sighed.

"At your age," groaned Randall.

"He's right, Preston. You been around too long to make a half-assed crack like that. How many sweet old ladies do you remember who took a meat cleaver to the garbage man? How many oh-so-refined good-looking gals who got busy with a knife on their boy-friends? Really."

I may have been losing professional status, but that was not important. What was important was to divert their attention away from any suggestion of a link between Louise and me.

"Yeah, I see what you mean."

I sat and waited.

By some mutual chemistry, which these two had developed over the years, they stood up at the same time.

"Might need a statement," intoned Randall.

"Always glad of a chance to help the law."

"H'm."

They went out.

I fingered the telephone, changed my mind, took my hand away. There might be some cops, some-where in the world, as smart as the two I'd just been talking to. If there are, I don't want to do business with them. If Rourke and his side-kick thought there was a one in fifty chance I was holding out on them, the telephone would be high on their list of little items requiring attention. I told Digby I was knocking off for the day, and left.

5

In order of places to be recommended to friends and visitors, pay-phones come low. They are full of broken glass, old chewing-gum and other assorted and undesirable pieces of flotsam. They also are plastered with invitations and messages of various kinds. Over the years, I have found it advisable to use the phone only in certain selected places.

Like Sam's.

Sam's telephone booths are always neat. They carry two bonus attractions. You can always see who's behind you, and you can also see that nobody is stealing your beer, or whatever. Nobody was behind me as I listened to the steady buzzing of Louise Carrington's private number. I checked in the mirror to see whether anybody was sampling my beer, again with a nil result.

I went back outside, took a pull at the ice-cold beer. Sam looked up as I waved a bill at him.

"A fistful of dollar. You wanta buy the place?"

"Change, Sam. I have to call a lady. She could take a lot of persuading."

He made change, took the bill, and bit gravely at one corner.

"Not that I don't trust you, Mr Preston."

I told him ha-ha, and went back to the grindstone.

"Anthony J. Holford, Attorney-at-Law. Can I help you?"

I wasn't going to go through all that again.

"Tell Mr Holford the call is from Monkton City. Tell him the name is Preston. Mark Preston. I don't want Mrs Stevens. I want Holford, and personally, and quick."

He came on within seconds.

"Mr Preston? I don't quite understand. I thought we had—"

"Not on this line, Mr Holford. Can you call me back on this number?"

I read from the plastic covered centre.

"Very well."

I figured if I was quick I might just have time for one more pull at that beer. Sam pretended not to be interested in my gymnastics.

The phone rang.

"Well now, who can that be?" said Sam, always the wit.

"If you must know, it's a lady wrestler I met. And she hates barkeeps."

I picked up the phone.

58

"Who is this?"

"I want to speak to Mr Preston. Mr Mark Preston."

"You got him, Mr Holford."

"Mr Preston, I am a very busy man. My cheque was sent to you, let me see, I can name the hour—"

"—No need, Mr Holford. Your cheque arrived and has been deposited."

Before he could expostulate further, I added, "and the amount was as we agreed."

"Oh." He sounded somewhat mollified. "Well, in that case, I don't see—"

"—Mr Holford," I interrupted again. "I needn't have called you at all. Our business has been concluded. It's just that something has come up. Something concerning our mutual friend. I thought you ought to know about it."

His tone went frosty.

"Something?" he queried. "What kind of something?"

Maybe it was the heat. I found myself getting exasperated.

"Look, Mr Holford, I could have left you holding this bag. And no skin off my nose. Do you want to hear about it or not?"

He thought about it.

"Well—" he began tentatively.

"All right. Our mutual friend has gone missing. But not merely missing. She has left behind one Arthur Flegenheimer, deceased."

There was a long silence at the other end.

"I don't believe we are really communicating, Mr

Preston. You said that Mr Flegenheimer is now deceased?"

"About as deceased as you can get," I confirmed. "He has three slugs in his chest, and is at present enjoying the benefits of one refrigerated slab down at the morgue."

More silence. I peeked in the mirror out of habit.

He said quietly, "Tell me, in your opinion, has Louise any connection with this?"

"I gave up having opinions about women long ago. Especially women who look like she does. But she isn't helping herself by hiding."

"No, no. Of course not. Do you think you might be able to find her?"

Fat chance.

"Don't waste your money, Mr Holford. I wouldn't know where to start."

"It was good of you to let me know, Mr Preston. I am in your debt. I shall have to contact her father at once and decide what is to be done. Goodbye."

Well, I'd done what I could. I cradled the phone, and was thoughtful as I resumed my position at the bar. There was no doubt that Louise Carrington could be in plenty of trouble. Her father drew a lot of water in my part of the world, but that wouldn't influence Rourke. If she had any connection with those holes in Stillman, the Irishman would find out, no matter how long it took. And whether she had or not, once the newspapers latched on to who she was, she'd get plenty of space.

I finished up my beer, told Sam so long, and went back to Parkside.

Once inside, I threw my coat on a chair and prepared myself for a quiet evening. I'd had about three minutes before the buzzer sounded.

I leaned one ear against the door and asked, "Who is it?"

"It's me, Louise Carrington. I have to see you, Mr Preston."

Oh, brother.

I opened the door.

She stood there, as beautiful as before, but with something else on her face. Fear? Worry? I couldn't tell.

"You'd better come in."

She came in quickly, nodding to me. Whatever was on her mind didn't prevent her inspecting the place with great interest. I've seen it before. Women have a tremendous absorption with the way a man lives by himself.

"And I clean my teeth, too," I assured her. "Night and morning."

She grinned.

"Sorry, I guess I'm just inquisitive."

"You'd better sit down, can I get you anything?"

"I'd love a glass of water please. I've been parked outside for more than an hour."

She drank it quickly, and with evident relish.

"More please."

This time she sipped slowly, and set the half-empty glass beside her.

"Thank you. I needed that."

Her hand went to her hair.

"The heat in that car was unbearable. I must look a mess."

I gave her an Old Favorite. She was not at ease, not the self-possessed woman I'd talked with at the Green Parrot.

"If this is the way you look when you're a mess, I must have a sight of you when you're all dressed up."

She smiled fleetingly, beginning to relax a little.

"It's nice here."

"It should be, the rent I pay."

I was in no hurry to get to the point. It suited me very well just to sit there, taking in those long, straight legs.

She began hesitantly.

"You must be wondering what I'm doing here."

"Just so you're here. Motives are secondary."

She fiddled nervously with her cigaret.

"I'm in trouble, Mr Preston."

"Better make it Mark," I advised. "What trouble?"

I wasn't sure in my own mind that I wanted to hear the answer. If this girl had killed Stillman, I would have no alternative but to give her to Rourke. And that thought was no part of my plans for Louise Carrington.

It all came out in a rush.

"Barney's dead. I went out to the club last night and he was dead. It was horrible. He was just sitting in his chair, and there was blood all over him. He seemed to be looking at me, as though it was my fault. He—"

"Hold on," I interrupted. "Just take it easy."

62

I fetched her another glass. This time there wasn't any water, just a fifty-year-old brandy I normally hide from visitors.

"Try this, and in sips. It isn't orange juice."

I guess it's breeding, or training, or something. She took the glass between her hands and rolled it around a few seconds. Then she held it to her nose.

"This is good."

"The idea is to sip it, not sniff it," I told her.

She smiled slightly.

'This illiterate character you try to portray," she observed, "he would not have brandy of this quality in the cupboard. He would have this year's genuine California brandy, and in the five-gallon can. This is nice."

She indulged herself sufficiently to let the stuff touch her lips.

"M'm."

There had been enough relaxation.

"Something about Barney?" I queried.

The glass hit the table with a bang.

She began to quiver. Long, shuddering tremors, that shook her whole body.

"He's dead. Horribly dead. And he was staring at me—"

I cut in.

"Yes. You told me that. But you have to bear in mind two important factors. One, this is none of my put-in. Two, there are policemen around, and you had better believe it is their put-in, who are very interested in your connection with this."

She stared, wide-eyed.

63

"But I haven't seen any policemen. I haven't seen anybody. How could you possibly—?"

Patiently I explained.

"Because they have been to see me. They had a theory that maybe I eased old Barney out of this bad world. They also asked me about you."

Silence.

Then, "About me? And why should they think you—?"

I held up a hand.

"Taking the second question first. They knew I was out at the Green Parrot the other night. They knew Stillman and I fell out about something, probably you. Guys, you may be surprised to learn, have killed other guys over women before."

She listened open-mouthed.

"But that's ridiculous. You hardly met me."

"They weren't to know that until they asked," I told her. "They're very interested in you, though. What are you going to do?"

She shook her head, dumbly.

"I don't know. That's why I'm here. I thought perhaps I could hire you to work for me."

I squinted.

"Work? Doing what?"

"I'm not quite sure. Yes I am. Two things. Prove that I didn't kill Barney, and find out who did."

Just like that.

"Well now, that's quite a menu you have there. Do you mind if I point out that nobody accused you of anything? And if anybody ever does, you need a lawyer, not a private detective. As to finding out who

64

did do it, let me tell you we have probably the best police force in the state. Why don't you try them?"

The shake of her head was decisive.

"I daren't. You know who my father is. This kind of publicity could do him a lot of harm. Won't you please help me?"

I fiddled with an ashtray.

"Would you want your father to know what I was doing?"

Silence.

Silence, plus a vacant kind of staring into space. Finally, she looked up, and her eyes met mine.

"No," she muttered. "No, I don't want him involved. Not if it can be avoided."

"H'm."

I thought it over, but my mind was really made up before I started.

"There would be conditions."

"Name them," she replied quickly.

"You're used to doing pretty well whatever you want. That was O.K. in that other world, the one outside. This is my world you're in now, and you'll be like a babe in arms. You will have to do exactly what I tell you, and all the time. I'm breaking the law in helping you. It doesn't worry me, I've done it before. But I'm used to my freedom, and I don't want to lose it because you won't obey orders."

She listened with a serious face.

"Yes, I can see that. I'll do as you say."

It sounded as though she meant it.

"You'll have to be honest with me. Tell me everything you know. No leaving things out because they're unpleasant, or might embarrass somebody."

"Very well."

I was satisfied.

"Tell me again about last night."

There wasn't much to it. She'd reached the Green Parrot at a little after eleven. There was a rear door, to which she had a key. Nobody saw her go into Stillman's office. She wasn't in the room more than two minutes at most. Then she ran out, again using the rear entrance, and went home.

"Why didn't you shout for help? Plenty of people in the club at that hour."

"I was scared out of my wits. I wasn't thinking at all. Just wanted to be away from there, away from—"

She broke off.

"So, as far as we know, nobody saw you there at all."

"Not that I know of."

Good and not good.

Good she wasn't seen, if that were true. Not good, she didn't scream the place down.

"Do you have a gun?"

"Heavens no. Whatever for?"

"Some women carry them around, just for protection."

She laughed nervously.

"I've been protecting myself since I was fourteen years old. And I never needed any gun."

I smoked in silence for a while.

"Well, from where I sit, you are in one jam. If you killed him, it doesn't need to be spelled out. But—"

66

and I had to raise a hand to still her immediate denial— "even if you didn't, you are still Louise Carrington, and that is not going to help your father's political career one scrap. Just that fact of your being involved with a character like Stillman would have taken a lot of playing down. But with a dead Stillman it is going to be a lot worse."

She nodded jerkily.

"Yes, yes, I know all that. Perhaps I've been a fool. But no more than that. What am I to do?"

What indeed? I sat and thought about it.

"People at the club. Roy, for instance, does he know who you are?"

"I don't think so. No, I'm sure he doesn't."

"Anybody else?"

She thought for a moment, creases on her forehead.

"No, I don't see how anybody could."

"H'm."

I leaned back and stared at the ceiling. There was no doubt in my mind as to what I should do. My clear duty was to pick up the telephone and call Rourke. Yes, I have her. Yes, she's here. Her name is Louise Carrington, you got that name—Carrington? Yes, she was at the club last night. I'll hold her till you get here. That was my clear duty.

Regrettably, duty does not always coincide with inclination. Here I had a frightened, worried girl, who may or may not hold the key to the Stillman rub-out. It was even possible she knew the truth, without being aware of it.

I knew what I was going to do. I also knew it was stupid, illegal, and had little chance of success.

She sat there, staring at me hopefully. Good old Preston, who was going to pull the rabbit out of the hat. Ha, ha.

"This is going to cost money," I told her. "Cash money, and handed over on the spot."

Her eyes clouded with disappointment. Reaching for her bag, she said stiffly, "Of course, I realise one has to pay for loyalty. How much do you need?"

It made me angry.

I got up from my chair, walked across and slapped her face. Hard. Twice.

"The money is not for me. I have to bribe people, buy people. I don't take money from women. Never had to. When I've done what needs to be done, you will get a proper bill from my office."

She held her face, where white patches showed on each cheek. She didn't seem to be frightened.

"You bastard," she spat. "When this is over—"

I pooh-poohed that.

"When this is over," I reminded her, "you will be free and clear, unless you're guilty. In which case, it will be a matter for the District Attorney, and not me. We had better understand one another, Louise. You are now on the wrong side of the fence, the side I understand. You will do what I tell you, and you will trust me. Because my neck is on the block, and I have a great regard for that neck. Goddammit, do you realise the simplest thing for me to do is to pick up that 'phone and turn you in? Do you realise the money I could be paid by the opposition newspapers, people who don't like your father, anyway? If we are going to work this out, if it can be worked out, then you are going to do exactly what I tell you. Any time, and all the time. Do I make myself clear?"

She rubbed ruefully at her face, silent for a few moments.

"Barney said you were a man to take seriously."

"That shows that Barney wasn't all fool," I agreed.

"I—I'm sorry for what I said. And I'll behave myself."

"O.K. Now we can get to work. You'll have to tell me everything you know about Stillman, his friends, his business, the works."

She began to talk.

6

SHE'D met Stillman a few weeks earlier at a party in Waldron City. He was a change from the young professional types she normally went around with, and in any case she'd practically grown up with most of them. He introduced her to a side of Waldron she had previously only read about in the newspapers. No fool, she suspected he was probably in the rackets, but the subject was never discussed, naturally. The past year or two she'd been increasingly restless with her way of life and had been toying with the idea of going away from her hometown, at least for a spell. I asked her if she ever took Stillman to her home.

She gave the ghost of a grin.

"Scarcely. Not that I'm worried about my father's opinions, so much. But it would not have been fair to him. I mean, if Barney really was up to something,

70

and was known to be visiting my father's house, you can imagine what the newspapers would do. You know, what's the phrase? Oh, yes. Known associate of racketeers."

"Did your father know about him?"

"Yes." She made a face. "We had a couple of spats about it, but that's not unusual. He and I don't get along too well. Haven't for some time."

And that was another story, which I was unlikely to hear.

"Go on about Stillman. Who were his friends or associates in Waldron?"

"No one in particular, so far as I know. He just seemed to know a lot of people. Everyone seemed pleased to see him, wherever we went."

"Tell me about coming to Monkton," I suggested.

"That. Well, it was all so casual. One evening he told me he'd be coming back here in a day or two. I simply said to him, 'O.K. I'll go with you.' It was that impetus I needed to break away."

"What did your father say?"

"Well, he raved a bit, but when he realised I wasn't going to move in with Barney, he calmed down. Besides, he knows there's no real point in arguing with me too much. If I say I'm going to do something, I don't often change my mind."

That I could believe.

"So you came?" I prompted.

"Yes. I moved into quite a reasonable apartment. In the mornings I'd mostly lie around on the beach. Barney works—um—worked very late and didn't get up till noon or one o'clock, you see. Then we'd have

71

some lunch and go out somewhere for the afternoon. In the evenings he'd go to the club and I would join him there at perhaps ten or eleven o'clock."

"Did he have many visitors?"

"Sometimes."

"Any names?"

"To be honest, he often introduced me, but I didn't retain the names. There wouldn't be any point."

I nodded.

"What kind of people?"

"The same kind we'd met in Waldron. You only had to look at them to know they weren't exactly surgeons or lawyers or anything like that. You know?"

I knew.

"What about Roy, where did he fit in?"

She shrugged.

"I could never quite work it out. He seemed to be a kind of personal assistant. If Barney wanted anything done, he always talked to Roy. I don't believe I ever saw any of Barney's other people go into his private office."

"Was there any particular telephone number that Barney called often?"

"Let me see."

She thought for a moment.

"Two. He bet on horses almost every day. I don't know the number."

"And the other?"

"That was a Wiltshire number. I don't know what it was."

Wiltshire. Movie territory.

72

"Do you know who he spoke to?"

"I know it was a man, but Barney never called him by name."

"Barney hardly spoke at all. He would say, 'Yes' 'O.K.' 'I see' 'I'll attend to it'. Non-commital things like that."

Not so non-commital. Stillman was talking to somebody in authority.

And that was all I could get. It wasn't a lot. A thought crossed my mind, a real long shot.

"Did Barney ever give you presents?"

"He was a very generous person. Always some little thing. Like, you know, perfume, a cigarette lighter and so forth."

"Nothing big?" I pressed.

"He did offer me a bracelet a few days ago, but it was too expensive. Solid platinum with diamonds inset. It's one thing accepting a twenty dollar bottle of perfume, but a girl has to know where to draw the line."

Check.

"What do I do now, Mark?"

That was what I'd been wondering while she'd been talking. I checked my watch. It was almost six-thirty.

"Getting late. It may not be possible to get everything done tonight. First we need a little help."

I picked up the telephone and dialled Florence Digby's home number.

73

7

AFTER arranging with La Digby that she would be at my place in about twenty minutes, I picked up the phone book.

"Who's Miss Digby?" enquired Louise.

"She's supposed to be my secretary. In fact she practically runs the whole operation. I'm not much on routine."

She looked worried.

"Why does someone else have to be involved? Surely the less people—?"

I wagged a stern finger at her. She stopped in mid-protest.

"All right," I sighed. "I'll go through it piece by piece."

I rested the phone book, and leaned against the wall.

"You are here, and I am here, and so far it's O.K. But it can't stay that way. Rourke—he's the homicide chief—he could be back tonight, tomorrow, anytime. Then he has us both. Right?"

A small nod.

"Conclusion, you have to leave. But you can't. I know Mr Rourke very well, and he is one smart copper. He doesn't leave out little details. Chances are he has a man out there watching to see what little tricks I get up to. And to see a girl who fits your description leaving Parkside with me living in it would be too much coincidence even for the dumbest flatfoot on the force."

"Yes, that makes sense. But also nonsense. You say I must leave here, but I can't."

"Right. Another girl leaves here. A girl with dark hair and glasses."

"Dark hair?"

She fingered at the honey blonde head.

"Yes. A wig. Personally, I don't keep too many around the apartment. Someone has to go and buy one. Now do you begin to see? If I went to get it myself, they'd probably holler for the Vice Squad. At the very least they'd remember me quite clearly. Conclusion, we need a woman."

She nodded vigorously.

"Oh, yes, yes. I'm beginning to feel better. I see it all now."

"No you don't. There's more."

She was all attention.

"Outside, one car. Your car. That's bad. The police may not have the number yet, but they soon

75

will. I would bet that within twenty-four hours, anybody driving around in that thing would be more
conspicuous than a naked woman riding a horse. We
have to get rid of it."

"But without a car—"

"You won't be without a car. We have to rent one.
Again, I can't do that Rourke would know within
the hour. You can't do it."

"I could give a false name," she suggested.

"True. But you can't give any false identification,
because you don't have any. Conclusion, Miss
Digby."

"Miss Digby is beginning to sound rather necessary."

I shook my head.

"Correction. Miss Digby is essential."

At that moment the buzzer sounded. The essential
Miss Digby had arrived.

She came into the room, carrying her forty plus
years like a thirty year old. She wore a blue linen
suit, with a little yellow collar. For the hundredth
time I wondered why somebody hadn't snapped her
up years ago.

The two women looked at each other appraisingly,
the way two strange women always do in that jungle
world of theirs.

"Miss Digby, this is Miss Louise Forrest."

They both said hallo.

I didn't like lying to the Digby, but it was necessary. If I turned out to be wrong about Louise, and
Florence knew her real identity when she helped her,

76

that would make her an accessory after the fact of murder. And I wasn't going to do that to Florence Digby for the sake of one small lie.

"Miss Forrest is in some danger. We have to hide her for a while."

I could see Louise was impressed with the calm reception this information drew.

Then I told Florence what had to be done. She was to rent a garage that locked, and get rid of Louise's car. Louise handed over the keys. Then she was to rent another car. There was the bit about the wig and the glasses.

I was at once interrupted by a five-minute discussion about wigs. Colour, style, the works. Finally, they reached agreement on these vital points and were ready to listen again.

The final job was to rent a room in a hotel. Tomorrow she would locate an apartment. She asked a few questions, all to the point.

"If I can use your phone I can fix the garage, the car, and the hotel right now."

"Go ahead. The book is open at car rental."

The car she booked in her own name, the other two as Louise Forrest. The whole job was done in fifteen minutes. We didn't speak, because Louise was naturally much too interested in every little detail. After all, it was her neck.

Florence cradled the receiver.

"Right," she said briskly. "I'll be off. Back as quickly as I can." Then most un-Digby like, "Try not to worry, dear. We'll do our best."

When she was gone, Louise said, "I like her. And she seems to know what she's doing."

"She's the best," I confirmed.

"I don't understand why she's not married though. She's very attractive."

What she meant was, is this the old movie about the boss and the secretary?

I laughed.

"Florence? Listen, when the refrigerator people want to bring out a new model, they sit around my office for days, studying Miss Digby."

We smiled.

"Now, there's the question of money," I resumed. "I can stake you, and you'll get a bill when this is all over."

Louise wagged her head sideways.

"No need. It was one of the first things I thought of, in case I had to run away. In here," she tapped at her purse, "I have two thousand five hundred dollars."

Good thinking. Very good.

"Well, that's one problem we don't have."

When Florence came back, she was all business.

"Car keys, two wigs, two pairs glasses. The car is a Ford, parked four slots to the left of the main entrance."

I wandered around with a drink while the women played wigs and glasses. When they were through, I studied the finished product. Except for the clothes, there was no more Louise Carrington, only Forrest. She was a striking brunette, the glasses covering

78

SOMEBODY HAS TO LOSE

enough of her face to make a man want to see
behind them. I gave her a wolf-whistle. Florence
frowned.

"The make-up is wrong for this colour, of course."

"Looks good to me."

"That's because you're only a man. Any woman
would know it at a glance."

I was suitably crushed.

"Will there be anything else, Mr Preston?"

"No, thank you, Miss Digby. I'm very grateful to
you."

"Not half as much as I am," interrupted Louise.
"Thanks a million."

La Digby thawed a trifle. She'd taken a liking to
this blonde/brunette who was in danger.

"Good luck, Miss Forrest. Perhaps we'll meet again
when this is all over."

Louise nodded emphatically.

"You can count on it. You're on the best dinner
they serve in this town."

Florence left. Louise turned to me.

"Well, I'd better go and find this hotel. I—I suppose you couldn't come with me?"

Regretfully, I shook my head.

"Sorry, honey. As I said before, there could be a
man out there. A pretty girl leaves, he'll take a good
look at her legs, give a deep sigh and get back to his
newspaper. But if that girl leaves with me, that makes
her more interesting. We don't want people interested
in you. Especially police people."

She was reluctant to leave, studying her appearance
in the mirror time and again.

"Am I really all right?" she asked nervously.

"You're fine. You'll have no trouble."

I could have wished all the fine manly conviction in my voice had been genuine.

"I—I like it much better here with you," she faltered. "I feel so safe with you."

"No chance," I said firmly. "You couldn't be in a less safe place, believe me. And, quite apart from everything else, I would have you know that no girl as edible as you is safe around me longer than, say, three minutes."

She smiled, felt a little better. She put a slim hand on my arm.

"You're nice. Maybe, when this is all over—"

The sentence did not require an ending.

"Maybe," I replied. "But the first thing is to get it over. Now," briskly. "Go straight to the hotel. Phone me the moment you get there. If you're hungry, have food sent up to the room. Stay out of sight. Florence will call in the morning when she's found an apartment. I'll be in touch as soon as I have anything, but mostly the contact will be from Florence. Got all that?"

"Right."

She perked up a little, took a final look in the mirror and picked up her bag.

"Secret Agent Forrest leaving on assignment."

I liked her guts.

"Do as I tell you, honey. We'll get out of this."

She nodded, and was gone.

Her perfume wasn't, the whole smell of her. Yes, maybe when it was all over.

80

SOMEBODY HAS TO LOSE

It seemed a long time till the phone rang. She was O.K. The room was comfortable, and she was a lot easier in her mind.

Well, that was one of us anyway.

8

IT WAS almost ten o'clock. I called the Green Parrot.
A man answered.

"Roy?"

"Yeah, who is this?"

"Preston."

"Preston who? Oh, I have you. The trouble maker.
What do you want?"

"I want to talk to you."

"We don't have anything to talk about."

His voice was guarded.

"You're wrong. There's plenty."

A pause while he thought it over.

"Make it quick, then."

"I don't talk well on telephones. They give me
nervous troubles. I want to come out there."

"You're barred."

"Uh-uh. That was by Barney. Old Barney isn't with us any more."

He thought about that one, too.

"Well, all right. But it better be good, and it better be short."

He hung up.

Rourke had been right about the .38. It was dirty. I spent a few minutes oiling and cleaning it, checking the mechanism. It would probably stay out of sight all night, but in my busines it pays to take these little precautions. After all, one man had died already.

Some people may think that murder would be bad for trade. Such people would be wrong. The car park at the Green Parrot was doing good business. In addition to the normal customers there were the gawkers, men and women both, who had made this trip out. Tomorrow they could tell their admiring listeners that they had dinner at the Green Parrot, 'You know, where that guy Stillman got bumped off'. This gave them an association with top hoodlums and racket characters. Some of them would claim to have known him. One or two of the men might even strut around cold-eyed for a day or so, snarling at anyone who spoke to them. It happened every time a half-world guy like Stillman cashed in.

The negro at the bar had to serve three people before he could get around to me.

"What'll it be, sir?"

"Let Roy know I'm here will you? Name of Preston."

He hesitated, lifted a gold telephone from behind the bar and spoke quietly.

"Mr Roy says will you have a drink. He won't keep you long."

I had a drink and looked around at the chattering bar. There was no music tonight.

"Excuse me, sir."

It seemed to be meant for me.

I turned to see a man about sixty plus years old with white fluffy side whiskers. He was medium height, and too fat.

"Me?"

"Yes. I wonder if I might speak with you?"

What harm? Maybe I'd learn something.

"What about?"

"Well, you see, I am a student of crime. Indeed I may say, yes I think I may say, I am somewhat of an expert on the subject."

One of those.

"And?"

"Well, sir, now please don't take offense, but I noticed that after you spoke to the bartender, he made a telephone call. I noticed further that you did not pay for your drink."

I debated whether to give him the brush, but he seemed a harmless old guy, and he was certainly excited. I decided to go along with him.

"What's it to you, pop?"

My voice was hard and cold. He loved it.

"I wonder whether perhaps you might have known the lamented Mr Stillman. Whether you could tell me something, anything about him."

I narrowed my eyes, and made him wait while I pushed an Old Favorite into my face and lit it. I left it between my lips, so that when I spoke, the words and cigaret smoke came out in equal parts.

"Sure I knew him."

My Brooklyn has never been very good, but it seemed to suffice.

"Splendid, splendid. Would it be your view that this is what is called a gangland rubout—"

Oh, brother.

"—or merely an isolated ordinary homicide."

An ordinary homicide, forsooth. My eyes by this time were so narrow I could hardly see through the slits.

"I don't know nothing about no gangland, whiskers. What I hear, they don't like it when people stick their fat noses where they don't belong. Me, I'm just a woiking stiff."

My coat accidentally fell open. He could just see the grip of the .38.

"Beat it."

"My word, oh my word."

He looked horrified, turned and scuttled back to a group of people on the other side of the room. He'd treasure this all his life. If he ever got around to writing a book, I would be immortalised.

Well, I reflected, I might not get the Academy Award, but I was sure of a nomination, even if only for childishness.

"What was all that about?"

Roy appeared beside me at the bar.

"The old boy wanted to know if I knew any gangsters," I told him.

"Another one," snorted Roy. "The place is stiff with those creeps."

"You could have bet on it," I assured him. "Happens every time after something like this. Five gets you ten Rourke already had four confessions."

He looked insulted.

"You think I'm an amateur or something?"

No, I don't think you're an amateur, I reflected. In my opinion you're a cool customer.

"Time is money," I reminded him. "Where do we talk?"

By way of a reply, he raised a flap on the counter, reached down and unlatched a small gate, pushed it open.

"Come on."

I followed him through, watched by the old guy and his party. They probably thought we were going to shoot it out in back.

There was a small room, about eight by eight, leading off the bar. The splendour outside was left behind. Bare walls, no window. Illumination was supplied by a single light bulb, dangling on a long flex. There were two chairs and a small table.

"Siddown."

Roy pulled out one of the chairs and parked. I followed suit. He'd picked his spot well. He would know that I would be immediately aware there was no intention to attack me. He'd left me the chair facing the entrance, so I would know I couldn't be surprised.

"So what's it all about?" he demanded.

I tapped my Old Favorite into an ashtray which invited me to drink Old Jock.

"Look," I opened, "I don't have any quarrel with you, not yet. All right, so you sicked the law onto me, but that was natural. You know they only have so many men, and the more leads they have to chase, the less chance they have to concentrate on any particular one. I'd probably have done the same."

He was listening intently.

"O.K., so you don't wanta fight. What do you want?"

"I want out. The cops have a tail on me—"

His eyes flashed as he interrupted.

"You mean you let those guys follow you out here? Are you crazy?"

I held up a hand.

"No, I don't mean that. I lost him back in Monkton. The point is, I'm in a very confidential business. To get information, anything which helps my clients, I'm not too particular about breaking a few laws. But I can't operate if there's some flatfoot behind me all the time."

"Tough. What do you expect me to do?"

I lit another cigaret before replying. It was hard to decide which tasted worse, the acrid smoke or the sweltering atmosphere in the windowless room.

"They have me tied up until this Stillman thing is finished. Way I see it, I'd better do what I can about that."

He put both hands on the table, leaned back and laughed aloud.

"I asked about you. One thing everybody was agreed about. You got one helluva nerve."

"Those are almost the very same words old Barney used the other night. You must have talked with the same people."

He stopped laughing. It had been an empty sound anyway.

"Never mind who I talked with. Just get outa here and don't bother to come back. You mess in this business, and you'll get lumps. Just for openers. This is none of your put-in."

I stared at him levelly.

"I think I might know where she is."

It stopped him cold. Some of his confidence dissipated.

"Where?"

I waved a finger.

"Oh, no. She's my only card. A very big card, but the only one. If I give her to you, I don't have a hand. Why, who knows, once they have her I might even wind up like dear old Barney."

I sat quietly while he thought over what I'd said. Before I said it, I hadn't the faintest idea whether Louise Carrington's whereabouts mattered a damn. I knew now. What I didn't know was what made her so important.

Roy drummed his manicured fingers on the table.

"You said something about 'they'. Who would 'they' be?"

"The guys who tell you what to do. I don't know all their names, I'll admit that."

"Just try me with a couple," he invited.

So there was a 'they'.

I chuckled.

"Oh, no. I know the way those guys operate. You don't get invited to any meeting of the board. You probably know only one of them, and he may be just a voice on the telephone."

Watching his face, I was almost sure I'd hit the spot. He was becoming less assured as the minutes ticked by.

"Look," I went on, "Your people will know I was here tonight. If you don't tell them, somebody out there will. Either one of the help, or one of the customers. They always take out that kind of insurance."

"So?"

But he knew the answer.

"They're going to want to know what I was doing here. They will already know we talked alone, and for exactly how many minutes. What will you say? That you gave me the bum's rush? Too late, even if you did it now. I've been in the joint nearly thirty minutes. So what was our conversation? It has to be about Stillman. You wouldn't want them to know that I almost offered a deal on the girl, and you wouldn't play. Roy, I think I'm wasting my time on you. I'm going to make a phone call, maybe I'll do better there. It's a Wiltshire number. I'll tell them you gave it to me."

I got up to leave.

"Wait." He motioned with his hand. "Siddown."

The fingers were now drawing nervous little circles on the table.

"You play rough."

89

I smiled at him pleasantly.

"It's a hard world."

Outwardly calm, I was beginning to feel the stir-rings of an old familiar excitement. When you start with nothing, like a poker game, then suddenly you get a hand that gives you a feeling you're up with the runners for that big jackpot.

"Why should you put me in a spot like this?" he demanded. "I'm nobody special. What I know don't amount to a row of beans."

"You're too modest, Roy. You know things I don't know. And that makes you special in my book. The other night you impressed me as a professional. I mean the gun bit and everything. Tonight you're jumpy. Oh, I know you're trying not to show it, but it's there. Why? You think you might be next in line for what Stillman got?"

For a moment I thought he wouldn't answer.

Then, "I don't know, and that's a fact. I don't even know why Barney got hit."

"Nor who did it?" I pressed.

"That either."

He could have been lying, but I had no way to be sure. I changed the subject.

"So what happens here now?"

"Huh?"

"I mean, have they sent a new Stillman, or did you get the job, or what?"

"No. I just have to run the joint as best I can, while they make up their minds what to do."

This was an important piece of information, if it was true. If 'they' had eliminated Barney, it would

90

not have been on the spur of the moment. People like 'they' didn't operate like that. It would have been well planned and timed. There wouldn't have been any question of them making up their minds what to do afterwards. That too would have been decided in advance, in precise detail. So, for the moment, I could assume that Stillman had been murdered by some third party, presumably for reasons which were not connected with 'their' business.

At that moment, the curtain was pulled partly open, and the barkeep stuck his head in.

"Sorry to interrupt, Mr Roy, but there's people here to see you."

"People?" queried Roy.

"Yeah, you know," the barkeep looked expressively in my direction, "People."

"O.K."

Roy got to his feet.

"I have to go. Do yourself and me a favor. Stay in here another five minutes, and then blow."

He went out. I was very interested in the new arrivals, and what they wanted. I did as Roy had asked and sat in the stifling little room, mulling over the handful of things I knew, and the trunkful I didn't.

Then I went out, but not away. Instead, I walked around the building to the back. We weren't having much moon tonight, and I kept a sharp watch for the inevitable row of garbage cans. If I bumped into those, it would sound like artillery fire in the still night.

I skirted carefully around each oblong of light

that came from a lighted window, staring quickly in as I passed. Finally I was outside the office where I'd talked with Stillman. There were two men standing facing the desk. I knew Roy had to be sitting behind it, but I couldn't see him because of the angle.

I studied the two. They were both over medium height, one thin and sad-faced. The other was broader and had a moustache. Laurel and Hardy would do by way of identification for the moment. They seemed to be arguing with Roy, but no words came through the thick glass. Roy didn't seem to be saying much, because there were very few seconds when either Laurel or Hardy wasn't talking.

These could be 'they' or at least have been sent by 'they'. Suddenly, they got tired of talking. The big one leaned across the desk, and heaved Roy out of his chair, I could see the back of his head now. While Oliver held him, Laurel sank two vicious punches into his lower middle. He couldn't collapse because of Oliver's grasp. Laurel hit him once more, then Hardy tossed him back into his chair, leaned across and slapped hard at his face, with an open palm. The party, I guessed, was over. I stepped well back into the shadows, just in time. The rear door opened, and a bright swathe of light cut into the night. They came out, closing the door. I wasn't thirty feet away, but I was safe. It would be many seconds before their irises adjusted to the dark.

There was a white Caddy parked close by the door. They got in. I made my way quickly to the Chev. As they rolled away, I followed, no lights. They turned towards Monkton City. I stayed a quarter of a mile behind, thankful for the gloom of the night, and praying I wouldn't be spotted by some motor-cycle cop. As we got closer to town, there was more traffic. I could put my light on now, without attracting their attention. I also got much closer behind, knowing how easy it is to lose a car in city traffic.

At the first main intersection they made a left turn. I didn't need to look at the sign to know what it said. It said 'Hollywood', and I liked it fine. Hollywood has plenty of Wiltshire telephone numbers. I hoped it was no mere coincidence.

9

THE roads were deserted now, unlit. The Caddy went round a sharp right bend. I was back a quarter mile again. As I turned the bend, there she was, parking sidewise across the road. I braked hard, stopping a few yards short of the white car. At once Laurel and Hardy appeared by my window. Laurel had a gun. He motioned me to roll down the window. The motor was still running. Maybe if I threw her into reverse and slammed my foot down, I could— No, I couldn't. I could never negotiate that bend in reverse, at speed. They'd thought of that one. Laurel waved impatiently. Sighing, I did what he wanted. Hardy leaned his head forward.

"O.K. What's it all about?"

His voice told me he wasn't the usual run of mug. I looked innocent.

94

"I don't get it. What's the gun for? You don't look like stick-up artists to me."

Hardy was impatient.

"Don't waste time. If that was our play, you'd be dead right now, and you know it. You followed us all the way from the Green Parrot. We want to know why."

"All that kid's stuff about no lights. What is this, the amateur hour?" grumbled Laurel.

If I kept acting innocent, they might get upset. Somebody might get hurt. Somebody like me.

"All right. I wanted to see where you went."

"Why? What's it to you?"

"It might help with something I'm working on."

They looked at each other.

"Working on, huh? Who are you, bucko?"

This from Laurel.

"Name is Preston."

"Ah."

They said it together. They'd heard the name before. Ignoring me, they talked to each other as though I wasn't there.

"What're we going to do with him?"

"We could bat him around a little, leave him here."

They thought about that one. So did I.

Finally Hardy said, "No, I think not. We have no instructions on this man. That rules out bumping him off, too. That's definitely out."

I was warming to this Hardy. Laurel's next contribution was, "We could let down his tyres. Take him

95

thirty minutes to do that job. We'd be fifty miles away."

"H'm."

Another silence while we all chewed that one over. It was the best idea I'd heard so far.

"Naw." Again from Hardy. "He's had a good look at us. He might holler copper, and then there'd be a sticker on us for highway holdup. Even if we squared that, certain parties wouldn't like it."

"Right."

"Why are you messing around in this, Preston?" asked Hardy.

"I have a vested interest," I replied. "The boys in Homicide think I know a lot about it."

"And do you?"

"Not much."

Laurel motioned his partner back a yard, and talked in low tones. From time to time they looked across at me. Then they seemed to have made up their minds. They came back to the car.

"O.K., you wanted to know where we were going. We'll take you there."

The world is full of surprises.

"Suits me," I shrugged.

"My buddy here will ride with you. Make sure you don't lose the way."

He turned and walked across to the Caddy. Laurel climbed into the back seat. Then, resting his weapon lightly on my head, he enquired, "Which side is it?"

"Under my left arm."

"You know how it's done."

Thumb and forefinger only, I withdrew the .38, and passed it back.

"Good. Flash your lights."

As I did so, the Caddy began to move away. Hardy drove slowly, so that any ideas I may have had about braking suddenly and throwing Laurel off balance could be forgotten. These two were the worst kind of tough guys. Tough guys come in many forms, but those who could think with it are very bad medicine indeed. And to meet two such, working together, was almost unheard of. It all seemed to point to one thing. There was something big in back of all this. Guys like Laurel and Hardy don't come cheap.

I wasn't too worried as I drove. They'd eliminated the idea of dealing with me physically. Then a nasty thought came into my mind. They had decided that because they had no orders. For all I knew we were going to see the man who gave out the orders. He might decide to issue some. And then I would be in trouble.

"Watch the left turn. You'll have to stop."

The Caddy made the turn. I slowed almost to a crawl as I followed him. We were on a single-track road. An elm tree had an illuminated board reading "Hurstville". An iron gate barred the road. The Cadillac stopped, and I pulled in behind it. A man dressed as much like a real police officer as he dared, appeared behind the gate. There was nothing of the imitation about the scatter gun he was carrying. He flashed a powerful beam into Hardy's face, snapped it off at once and opened the gate.

"Move up about five yards," I was told.

I did so, and Scatter Gun came over with his light.

"No names," shouted Laurel from the back.

"Oh, it's you. Who's your friend?"

"Never mind. Tell them at the house there's one more for bridge."

"Kay."

He stood back to let us pass, then walked away to some hidden phone.

The road was almost a half-mile long. I began to pass through lawns, tennis courts. There was a swimming pool, fully lit, but devoid of custom.

Then came the house. I've never actually seen the Palace of Versailles, but this came pretty close to it.

"Cosy little place," I observed.

Laurel tittered.

"Yeah. And that's only where the butler lives."

Jokes yet.

"There's a car park in back. Take that turn there."

I took that turn there. The car park was good for fifty at a guess. The Cadillac was neatly parked among the white markings, with Hardy standing waiting. I rolled in beside him and stopped. We got out.

"Any trouble?"

"Nope. He had this."

"This" was my .38. Hardy took it, hefted it in his hand.

"Nice," he commented. "Police Special isn't it?"

"It is."

"Nice," he repeated, sticking the gun in his pocket. "Come on."

SOMEBODY HAS TO LOSE

We went up wide marble steps to the back of the house. There were several pairs of french doors. Hardy ignored these, settling for a plain door leading into a narrow passage. This would be where the work was done. The kitchen, freeze area, wine-stores and so forth. At the end Hardy opened a door on the right, motioned me in.

"You wait in here. We won't be long. Don't even think of doing anything foolish. Oh—and have a drink if you want."

The door was locked, and they went away. The room was medium size, and cold. I didn't have to look very far to understand why. The walls were lined, floor to ceiling on three sides with cartons, crates and other containers of every variety of spirit known to man. The fourth wall was devoted to the wine-racks. By way of passing the time, I made the best calculation I could of the value of the stock. Quick pencilled notes on the side of one of the cardboard cartons took about fifteen minutes to complete and total. Although no expert, I was confident of being wrong by not more than a thousand or two either way. My total was just under twenty-five thousand dollars. That is a lot of drinking by anybody's standard. Another rough calculation told me I would take a minimum of twelve years to drink it all, and even this was offset by the chilling knowledge that if I tried I would in any case be dead within five.

By now, the cold was beginning to get to me. It wasn't below freezing, but I was dressed for the outdoor night air, a clear twenty degrees warmer than this cold-room. Although I had dismissed Hardy's invitation as being his little joke, I now found myself looking hungrily at the serried ranks of warmth bringers. Why not? The guy could afford it.

I ran stiffening fingers along the cartons, searching my memory, not so much for palatability and smoothness, but rather for instant warmth. And there it was. A splendid malt, all the way from the Highlands. Jock's Joy.

Opening it was no problem. There was a small rack with every type of opener I've ever known, plus a few I hadn't seen before. But a glass was a different problem. There was nothing, not even a plastic cup. My teeth were beginning to chatter. Finally, I found a box of funnels. Silver, naturally. I selected the smallest, held a forefinger over the tip, and poured in some Jock's Joy. I contrived with two shaking hands to raise the funnel to my lips, and took a great gulp of the amber liquid.

I stood still and waited. It began to spread through me. The cold seemed to be arrested for a few moments. I took another drink. The cold hesitated, then began to retreat. I felt the tingling in my feet, then moving all through me, down my arms, and into my hands, which had been shaking only a few seconds before. My finger-stopped funnel was empty. I picked up the bottle, was about to pour, and stopped.

I had taken a drink, a large drink, to fend off the cold. That was allowable. Any further drinking would be for pleasure, and that was off limits. Soon, at least I hoped it would be soon, the two comedians would be back for me. Moving out of that cold-room into a normal, well-heated atmosphere could well be too much for me if I'd become too chummy with man's only friend, Jock's Joy. With reluctance, I rammed home the stopper, put the bottle down. I stomped around, slapping at myself, circulation improving by the second. I even managed to light an Old Favorite, pulling the smoke down gratefully, to where it would do the maximum of damage. Warm again, I began to look for practical aids. I must have walked past them a dozen times before their import-ance hit me.

Ice-picks.

A whole row. Ranging from about three inches to ten in length. I took a three-inch, slipped it under the strap of my watch. Fine. As long as I didn't bend my wrist, it would not stick into my flesh. Next I selected a nine-inch, a vicious piece of tooling, which I stuck into my waistband. No good. The point stuck into my leg when I walked. I would have to manage without it. No, I wouldn't. There were corks everywhere. Withdrawing the pick, I stuck the point firmly into a robust cork. Then I tried the waistband again. This time, no problem.

I felt better. Not only was I armed, always a comfort, but I was dealing with people who were confident I was not. I had two strikes on them. A few more minutes went by, and Jock's Joy was in danger again, when I suddenly heard the key turn.

The door opened and there was Hardy.

"This way," he grunted.

When I felt the comparative heat of the corridor,

I was glad I'd taken it easy on the malt. There was a door at the end, leading into a large hallway.

Instead of the usual Hollywood baroque I'd been expecting, the furnishing and decor were restful. Restful and expensive. There was a curving stairway leading to the upper floor, which could have been veined marble, and probably was. Hardy knocked on a heavy oak door, opened it and pointed me inside.

This would be the library. You can always tell the library, because it has rows and rows of leather bound, hand tooled, unread volumes in sets.

A man sat behind an enormous desk. Standing, I would guess him to be about five ten, and slim with it. He was about fifty years old, immaculately dressed, and with recently barbered gray hair.

He watched me approach.

"Mr Preston, is it not?"

The voice was that of a cultured man. He was Ivy League plus. I didn't know what to make of the set-up. Hardy went and stood by a window. Laurel was already there.

"It is," I admitted.

"Mr Preston, you seem to be interesting yourself in my affairs. Is one permitted to ask why?"

I liked his style. 'Is one permitted' indeed. What he meant was, his goons would kick in my teeth if I didn't come across. I grinned.

"Whoever you are, you got some style there."

Nobody asked me to sit, so I went and grabbed a fragile-looking chair with gold lacquered arms, lifted it in front of the desk, and parked. Laurel and Hardy looked at the boss, but he merely lifted one finger.

"Yup," I continued, "style. You say I'm interested in your affairs. You may be right, but you have to have one thing in mind."

"And what might that be, Mr Preston? And, by the way, please sit down."

I chuckled.

"Thanks. I don't know what your affairs are. Now, you tell me that, and I'll tell you if I'm interested. O.K.?"

He smiled wryly. For all his voice, clothes and surroundings, I decided this was a very tough egg.

"My affairs are widespread, Mr Preston. I could not presume to bore you with all the minute details. However, since you persist in your role of illiterate lout, which I may say is a waste of time, let us concentrate on one small fact. You were following my associates. Why?"

"To see where they were going," I told him.

He made a gesture of annoyance.

"Come, come, Mr Preston. This is not leading us anywhere. At present, I have nothing against you. Frankly, I don't even find you very interesting. Simply explain yourself, and you could be leaving here in five minutes."

Well, as long as we were talking, nobody was bouncing anyone around.

"They were at the Green Parrot."

He raised an eyebrow.

"A public place, I understand?"

I shook my head.

"Not where they were. They were in the manager's office, slapping him around."

103

I felt Laurel and Hardy stir restlessly, but did not take my eyes off the head man. His voice was icy calm.

"How do you know this? Were you in the room?"

"No," I admitted. "I was watching through the window."

"Ah."

He moved an ashtray, while he thought it over. Blue, green and yellow lights flashed from the cut glass as he did so. The sight of the ashtray prompted me to feel for my Old Favorites. A quick burning pain at my wrist reminded me that the icepick was there. I moved my hand more gingerly.

"I'm afraid I must ask you to explain a little more, Mr Preston. Even supposing what you say is true, supposing these gentlemen had a difference of view with the manager, why should that interest you?"

He stared at me enquiringly.

"Because I want to know who knocked off Stillman."

He nodded understandingly.

"Really? Why?"

I got all confidential.

"Homicide have me down for a piece of the action, that's why. Oh, I don't mean they think I killed him. At least, I don't think that's what they think. But they have a theory I know more than I'm telling. Every time I open a drawer, a flatfoot falls out. In my business, coppers are very bad news. You see, the reason people come to me is because they can't or won't go to the law. If the law is crawling all over my carpet, the customers stay away. I don't operate.

104

If this Stillman thing isn't cleared up, I'm in real danger of having to look for honest work."

"H'm. And that is why you were at the Green Parrot?"

"Right. I figured there was a chance I might learn something. Then, when Laurel and Hardy turned up—"

"Laurel and Hardy?"

He sounded mystified.

"Yeah. These two."

I jerked a thumb at them.

For once he took his eyes away from me, to inspect the two men by the curtains. They didn't seem to think it was funny.

"Laurel and Hardy," he repeated, chuckling. "Oh, yes, very good. Pray continue."

"That's all. They were no ordinary customers, because they went into the business area. Then they started pushing Roy around. To me, that made them interesting. They were all I had, so I followed them."

He sat and digested this.

"What you say is just sufficiently unconvincing to be the probable truth. I believe I'm going to be frank with you, Mr Preston."

Well, it had been a long time since anybody told me a fairy story.

"Why?" I wanted to know.

"Why?" he repeated.

"Yeah, why? You're holding all the cards. These comedians have my gun, I'm a thousand miles from anywhere. Nobody knows I'm here. You could have me buried out in those woods inside an hour. Why tell me anything?"

He held up both hands in mock horror.

"My dear Mr Preston, such melodramatics. You really will have to curtail your television viewing. You are in no danger here. When we've had our little chat, you will be quite free to go. The reason I choose to tell you certain things is so that you will understand that our interests do not conflict. You will then realise that my affairs are no concern of yours, and you will cease to be a nuisance, however small."

I liked the part about being free to go. Now for the bedtime story.

"I too, am very interested in the late Mr Stillman. You see, he had some property of mine, which he was holding for me. It is missing, and I want it back. There are three possibilities. The person who shot him has it. One of the club helpers took it after he was killed. The police found it while investigating."

"Four," I followed on. "You had him bumped off because he wouldn't come across."

His words were like drips of ice.

"I don't want to have to tell you again about that imagination, Mr Preston."

"Ah," I scoffed. "Imagination? These hoodlums bring me out here under a gun. That's imagination? Oh, I know they're very high-class hoodlums, but hoodlums just the same. And you, for all your Fancy Dan, are a tough character. I've met guys like you before. People look at the clothes, listen to the voice, not to mention the dialogue. They put you down as some kind of executive, or an art-collector or some-

106

thing. Nobody to worry about. Well, I'll tell you this. You don't fool me. I worry about you."

He heard me out.

"I have heard of you in the past. Among other things, I know you to be a person of some judgement, which is an asset. I also know you sometimes are unable to curb your tongue, and this is on the debit side. Let us hope you will not have cause to worry about me."

I hoped so too.

"O.K. Suppose I go along with the missing treasure bit. Would it be worth somebody's trouble to shoot old Barney to get their hands on it?"

"Very much so. It is worth a great deal of money."

"What is it, anyway?"

He sighed.

"Really, Mr Preston. I'm afraid I can't discuss that."

I reflected before speaking again.

"Let's suppose, just suppose, I bump into this sea-chest or whatever while I'm roaming around. That ought to be worth a little something."

He placed his open hands along each side of his nose.

"Perhaps. In the unlikely event of your finding such a thing, we should have to discuss such little details at that time."

I shifted in the narrow chair.

"How'll I get in touch with you?"

"By the simple expedient of picking up a telephone."

He leaned across the desk and placed a small white

card in front of me. The lettering was in gold, naturally. The legend read "Art-World Inc." There was a telephone number, a Wiltshire number.

"There's no name," I pointed out.

"Certainly not. Those are for my employees to use. People in my position have no need of such things. However, there is no reason for me to be mysterious with you, Mr Preston. I am Grover J. Mitchell."

It was obviously intended to have an effect. The name was faintly familiar, but only faintly. I didn't want to hurt his feelings, not right at that moment, so I looked impressed.

"Well, well," I well-welled. "O.K. Mr Mitchell, if I come up with this stuff of yours, I'll be in touch."

I slipped the card into my pocket.

"One more thing," I added. "I'm having enough trouble shaking coppers out of my coat tails. I don't want to find these guys in there as well."

He nodded slowly.

"Agreed. At the risk of wounding your feelings, I must tell you that I don't consider your little activities either interesting or important enough to justify my spending any money on you."

It's nice to be appreciated. I got up. Laurel and Hardy became immediately alert.

"Just to show my heart's in the right place, I'm returning some of your property. It doesn't seem I'm going to need it."

I removed the small ice-pick from my wrist and laid it in front of him. Reaching inside the waistband of my pants, I hauled out the big one, and placed it alongside its little brother.

108

"Sign of good faith," I explained.

Laurel shifted uncomfortably, while Hardy's face reddened. Mitchell's eyes flickered swiftly over them, came back to me. He laughed as though he meant it.

"I like a man of some resource," he chuckled. "There is not perchance an army rifle strapped to your leg?"

"I had to stop doing that," I explained. "It made me walk too stiffly."

But I knew my two old buddies hadn't heard the last of the ice-picks.

"Show him out," said Mitchell. "Goodnight, Mr Preston."

The audience was ended. We went out into the dark night.

They walked with me to the car, saying nothing.

"About the gun?"

Hardy reached in his pocket, and handed it over.

"You wouldn't want to sell it?"

"We've been together too long," I told him.

They watched as I backed around and drove away. At the end of the drive, the gate stood open. There was no sign of the guard.

I had still not identified Grover J. Mitchell by the time I got back to town.

10

I PARKED outside the offices of the Monkton City *Globe*, and went in. The night editor was Shad Steiner, an old friend, and one of the sharpest news-hawks on the coast. This was his busy time, and I could imagine how delighted he was going to be when I walked in. I saw him first, through the grimy glass walls of the cubicle grandly titled 'Editor'. The desk seemed to be in chaos as usual, and people kept running in and out. Out of all the disorder would emerge a nice tidy newspaper right on the deadline.

Steiner didn't look up when I went in, but simply held out a hand. When I put nothing in it, he snapped his fingers, with the same result. That made him look up.

"What the— Oh, no. Go 'way."

"If you're busy, Shad, I can wait."

He threw up his arms.

"Busy? Why would I be busy? I have five pages all buttoned up already. That leaves a mere nineteen to be done, and I have all of three hours left. Of which I shall be honoured to give you precisely one minute."

I grinned at the irascible old face.

"I want to get at the morgue."

"Why?"

"There's an outfit called Art-World Inc. Want to see what you have on them."

If possible, the wrinkled brow contrived to add another furrow.

"Art-World," he repeated. "Movie people?"

"Could be."

He pushed a button, and hollered.

"Freddie, get in here will you?" Then to me, "You're in luck. The movie man covered an opening tonight. Just writing it up. Don't keep him too long, huh? He always writes fifteen hundred, knowing damn well I have to cut it back to five."

A youngish man came in, looked at me curiously.

"Freddie, this is Mark Preston. Claims to be some kind of detective. Take him away, where he can't bother me. Tell him whatever he wants to know. And if he needs the morgue, that's O.K. too."

"Thanks, Shad. See you."

"Not tonight you won't."

I followed Freddie out. There was a room with four or five shirt-sleeved, sweating men, banging on typewriters. Every now and then one would shout out the tribal cry "Copy".

Freddie said, "This is where I work. Guess it's a little noisy, huh?"

"A little," I agreed.

"I think Features may have gone home," he mused. "They don't get much last-minute stuff. This way."

We went down a small passage and he opened a door.

"Yeah, this'll do."

We went in. He parked behind one of the two desks. I grabbed a chair.

"That right, you're a detective?"

"That's what I claim. Private."

He was interested.

"A real one. This is great. I've seen so many movies about you guys. I was beginning to think Hollywood invented you."

"Not quite."

I held out my Old Favorites, but he didn't smoke.

"You must be pretty good," he went on. "Old Steiner doesn't take night staff off the grindstone, and tell them to open the morgue for anybody who walks in."

He let it hang there. A kind of invitation for me to recount my hair-raising exploits. Not tonight, brother.

"We're old friends," I explained. "I'm trying to find out something about an outfit called Art-World Inc. Does it ring any bells?"

He didn't even pause to think. I'd got the right man.

"Art-World? I should just think so. The hours I've

112

spent watching their crap. It got so bad that in the end I protested to the Chief Editor, and he agreed I needn't bother any more."

Unusual, I would have thought.

"What kind of crap? I mean, what makes them unique?"

He made a face.

"Well, you take the real companies. Take Warners, M.G.M. and the rest. They make real movies. Art-World make yuck. I think the last one was called 'Sex and the Teenage Martians'. You get the drift?"

"Oh, those."

"Yeah, those. You wouldn't think they could survive with such junk. The fact is, Mr Preston, second string theatres all over this great nation actually screen these pictures, and people go to see them. Also, they're very big in South America and some of the Asian countries. They splash out maybe two hundred thousand, and expect an average five for one return. And they make a lot of pictures."

"Nice odds," I commented.

"And that isn't all, I hear." He looked at me quizzically. "Are you a talkative man, Mr Preston?"

"Only when I want to be."

"Don't misunderstand me, but Mr Steiner is very strict about one thing in particular. We don't print any H.R. and G. It's a golden rule. But it doesn't stop us hearing things."

"H.R. and G?"

I wasn't pretending when I sounded mystified.

"Sorry, newspaper shorthand. Hearsay, rumour and gossip. Mr Steiner says the terrible three have

113

ruined more lives than you could count. The *Globe* will not be adding to the total."

It sounded like Shad.

"He could be right," I agreed. "Still, since we're not printing anything, do we have any—er—H.R. and G. on Art-World?"

"We do, we most certainly do. For one thing, the casts of their pictures are always unknowns. They are careful to select people who are almost certain not to make it. They are always young, beautiful—including the men—but they lack any real talent. Art-World signs 'em up, on a salary per picture basis. Any options are only available to the company. The kids sign. They'll sign anything to see themselves up on that big screen. Anyway, didn't their agent say it was O.K.? What they don't know is, these so-called agents are outriders for Art-World themselves."

"So," I mused, "if I'm following you, if you don't happen to be working on a picture at the moment, you don't eat."

"You got it. There's no retainer. And no way to break the contract. It's all nice and legal."

I picked my words carefully before speaking again.

"No offence, Freddie, but for a film critic, you seem to be unusually well-informed about things which I wouldn't have thought would come your way. Mind if I ask why?"

He shrugged.

"You're right. I do know a lot, but I can't claim the credits. Some time ago, maybe a year, one of these kids came to the paper with a story. She wanted some help to break away from these ghouls, and naturally hadn't any money for lawyers. Well, we had our legal eagles go into the contract. I'm told they even put it under the microscope. Believe me, ours boys are the best. If there had been one punctuation mark out of place, they would have found it. But no dice. The girl told us a lot of other things, too. Nothing we could pin down to hard facts. Nothing we could prove. We all felt bad about the kid, but there wasn't a thing we could print."

"H.R. and G.?"

"Check."

Perhaps if I found the girl, I was thinking. H.R. and G. might be off limits to the *Globe* staff, but they were the breath of life to people in my line of business.

"Do you happen to remember the girl's name?" I wondered.

"Not off-hand. Gloria something. I could look it up."

"Maybe if I talked with her, I could come up with something. Not something you could use, but—"

My voice trailed away, as I watched his head wag from side to side.

"She was murdered a few weeks later. We were allowed to print that one."

His voice was bitter. He was blaming himself, and the *Globe*, for the girl's death. Closed file.

"Oh. You mentioned something about other things she told you. Do you recall what they were?"

"Very clearly. She'd made exactly one picture, months before she came to us. I think this epic was called 'The Fiend who Feasted on Girls'. Since then, nothing. That's when Art-World started to close in. The big director, Bart somebody, was interested in her for a picture he was casting. Man like that could do a lot for Gloria. Of course, she'd have to be reasonable. Plenty of others who would jump at the chance."

"I have the scene," I rejoined. "And she went for it?"

"She was hungry, Mr Preston. People will do a lot of things when there's nothing under the old belt."

No argument there. I thought about Grover J. Mitchell, sitting out in his fairy castle, well clear of all the dirt and grime of his little empire.

"They sound like nice people," I said reflectively.

"That isn't all," he countered. "You want more?"

"I want it all."

Freddie sat further back in his chair.

"Sometimes they get another movie. The first one, the one where their name goes up outside the theatre, is pretty bad, but not so bad it won't pass the censors. The second one, if they get that lucky, is not quite in that bracket."

"Blue movies," I muttered unnecessarily.

"Big market for the stuff. You see, most of these creepy-crawlies are made in warehouses, empty buildings. They're not properly equipped or lit, and the end product shows it. Plus, they are not made by movie people, not people with real live studio experience. Again, it shows. Of course, you do get the occasional professional, somebody who got the bum's rush from Dream City for getting loaded once too

116

often on the job. But even he can only work with what he has."

"I imagine you're going on to say that Art-World produce an obvious pro job, because all the facilities are there?"

"Right. It's a perfect set-up. The little guys, the back-street operators, have to have lookouts posted hither and thither, in case the law shows up. This gives them enough time to get clothes on the players, but that's about all. They can't hide cameras, arc lamps and the rest of the bric-a-brac. But a real studio, like Art-World, they don't need to hide anything. All that equipment is part of their legitimate business. If the Vice and Morals did decide to take a look, they have to stop at the gate. The guard lets them through, presses his alarm bell. By the time the police get to the shooting studio, the red light is on. They have to wait a few minutes, because even the dumbest country boy knows the red light means strictly no admittance, not even to the President of the company. Finally, they get inside. The film on the floor is Scene 6, Sex King of Venus. They go away empty handed, and with a warning that the Chief of Police is going to hear about their behaviour."

Art-World was beginning to sound like a tough nut to crack. If I even wanted to try. I was by no means certain their business, crummy as it was, was any of my put-in. My only concern was to find out who killed Stillman, and to get Louise Carrington off the hook.

"What do you know about Grover J. Mitchell?" I asked him.

Freddie's eyes widened.

"You've been busy, Mr Preston. Some people even work for Art-World, and they never heard the name. How'd you pick it up? That is, if it's not confidential of course."

He added the last part all in a rush, careful of my professional integrity.

"No secret," I assured him. "I was out at his house tonight. We had a little chat."

If his eyes went any wider, I'd swear they were going to pop out.

"Nobody, but nobody gets in there. How'd you do it?"

"I had a couple of people with me. His people. They thought I ought to see him. And they had nasty guns, so I went."

Freddie looked suspicious.

"You've been taking me for a ride. You knew all this before you came in here. Are you wasting my time, Mr Preston?"

"Believe me, no. I didn't even know what Art-World Inc. did for a crust until you told me. What I've heard these last fifteen minutes is all bonus to me."

He was mollified.

"So your business with him was connected with something else?" he prompted.

"Correct. And I'm sorry, Freddie, but that part of it stays under wraps."

"S'O.K. I understand."

But he was disappointed.

"Does the name Stillman mean anything to you?"

118

He placed a forefinger on the tip of his nose, muttering "Stillman." After a few seconds he said, "Sorry, no Stillman. What's his part?"

"I wish I knew," I confessed. "Anyway, his part, if he had one, has been brought to an end. Somebody got careless with three heavy shells. They left them in his chest. You know, Freddie, you ought to take an occasional peek at this newspaper of yours. The Stillman kill was right on page one just a few days ago."

He chuckled.

"You're right. By the time I've gotten through the sports pages, I'm too tired to look at the rest. I'll read up on Stillman."

"One more thing," I requested. "You said these so-called agents are really front men for Art-World although they seem to act as independents."

"Yup, that's right."

"Do you think you could dig up the name of the guy who signed up your friend Gloria?"

"Can do."

And quite suddenly I had a thought. There was no rhyme or reason behind my next question.

"There's another girl. Name of Elaine Evans. She was murdered little over a month ago. Could you dig around on her, see if there was any connection, anything at all, with Art-World?"

He looked doubtful.

"Well look, Mr Preston. I can certainly try, and I'll be glad to help you, but it could take an hour or more. I have to file my copy, and soon, or Mr

119

Steiner will be tearing out hair. My hair. Would tomorrow be O.K.?"

It was time to go home. I got up.

"That'll be fine. You've told me a great deal, I appreciate it. Shall I call you tomorrow?"

"Well, maybe not. I'm never certain what time I'm going to wake up. Better let me call you."

"Fine."

We shook hands, and I went out.

I looked in on Shad, but he was too engrossed in his work. Outside, the night air was chilling off at last.

I went home for a shower and bed.

11

IT WAS an uneasy, disturbed night. One time I was with Louise in the booze-room at Grover J. Mitchell's house. Then Mitchell came in and started throwing ice-picks at me as if I were a dartboard. Next, I was running down a long, dark street, while Laurel and Hardy slowly gained on me. I didn't have to be told what was going to happen when they caught up. Lawyer Holford was sitting under a street-lamp, writing cheques. He tut-tutted as I went by. Then he pulled out a sub-machine gun and proceeded to mow down the thin man and the fat one. Only it wasn't them at all. It was Rourke and Randall. I never saw the end of it, maybe I went into a real sleep. It couldn't have been for long. When I woke up I felt like the man in the ads before he takes the miracle cure. Nearest thing I stock to the miracle cure is coffee and Old Favorites, so I got busy on both.

121

An hour later I walked into the office. Florence Digby's desk was neat and untenanted. I frowned. It was ten in the morning, and La Digby was nothing if not punctual. I went through into my own room and found a note on the desk.

"I need a new apartment."

Then I remembered. She had to get Louise fixed up. Good. There was a small pile of mail by my right hand, but I let it lie. The sharks and my sex problems could wait.

The telephone shrilled. It was La Digby.

"Oh, Mr Preston, I have arranged that matter. I should be at the office in about one hour."

Remembering a story I once read about phone-tapping, I said, "Thank you, Miss Digby. You realise I shall have to deduct one hour's pay from your salary."

"Naturally, Mr Preston. I would expect nothing else."

I held a cold phone.

Sometimes I wake at night, wondering what would happen to me if I ever lost Florence Digby. On such nights I seldom sleep well afterwards.

One Old Favorite later the phone clacked again.

"Mr Preston?"

I admitted it.

"This is Freddie. From the *Globe*. We talked last night."

The fog cleared.

"Yeah. Sure, Freddie. What did you find out? And how come you're up so early?"

122

"I'm not up, Mr Preston. Not the way you mean. I haven't been to bed yet."

He did sound kind of weary.

"So what's the story?"

"It's like this. When I wrapped up the paper, I kept on thinking about you. I knew it wasn't any use going home till I settled my mind."

I flicked ash from a new cigaret.

"You mean about those two girls? Elaine Evans and Gloria Somebody."

"No," he contradicted, "I mean about you. Trouble with my job is, a man tends to specialise. You know, keep on one narrow track without looking to either side. But your name kept nagging at me. I had to look up your track record."

"That should have kept you busy for quite a while," I contributed.

"You'd better believe it. And that last one, that was a lulu."

I pondered.

"Which last one are we talking about?"

"That Butterworth case." *

I stared out of the window. A man in a cream Olds was having a slanging match with a traffic cop.

"O.K., so I'll mail you my autograph. What is this, Preston Day?"

He sounded hurt.

"Well, hell, you did ask me to help you."

"Sure. I'm sorry, Freddie. It's just my secretary didn't show for work, and that upsets my whole day.

* They Call It Murder.

So, apart from learning what a fine upstanding citizen I happen to be, did you find out anything else?"

His voice sounded as though he was somewhat mollified.

"Well, yes. It isn't much I'm afraid. I drew a short straw on the girl Gloria. But I do know the agent who was Elaine Evans's personal representative."

Well, that was better than nothing. I picked up a pencil and drew a pad towards me.

"Could be a lead there," I told him, trying to sound like a man who believed there could be a lead there. "Who was he?"

"He was, and is, a man named Arnie Halliday. You want the address?"

"If you have it."

He not only had it, but he had the telephone number too. He would probably supply the guy's physical description and number of kids if I'd let him go on, but I had all I needed.

Finally, I managed to stop the flow, thanked him profusely and hung up.

Arnie Halliday.

I sat, and racked around in my mind. No Halliday. Finally, I picked up the phone and dialled.

A cooing type female voice answered.

"Halliday Enterprises. Can I help you?"

"You can, miss. Put me through to Halliday."

There was a shocked silence.

"Mr Halliday?"

"The same," I confirmed.

"Why, that's out of the question. I mean—"

"I know what you mean," I assured her. "Just tell

124

him that a man named Preston, that is Deputy Sheriff Preston, will be there at twelve noon. If Mr Halliday knows what's good for him, he will be available. You got that?"

Another agonised pause.

Then, "Did you say Deputy Sheriff?"

"I did. You tell him. Twelve noon. And he'd better be there."

Having said what I wanted, there was no point in prolonging the conversation. I cradled the phone.

I hadn't thought it necessary to elaborate on the details. The Deputy Sheriff gag was something that happened a long time ago. It had been some caper in Jerkwater, Nebraska, or maybe Goonville, Ohio, the place escapes me. For services rendered, like finding a candy-bar the mayor's kid had mislaid, I was made an honorary Deputy Sheriff on the spot, and I still had an official looking badge to prove it.

With my foot well down, it took me twenty-five minutes to reach the building where Halliday did whatever he did. I parked in a reserved slot. A tough looking character materialised from nowhere. He surveyed me with disdain.

"What's up, buddy? You can't read?"

I grinned at him wolfishly.

"Nice bridge work," I complimented. "You wanta keep it?"

Then I flashed the Deputy Sheriff shield from Slobtown, Oregon, or wherever it was. He went quiet.

"Now, if anything happens to the car, I am going to come looking for you. Personally. You got that?"

"O.K. officer. I got it."

125

I gave him one of those hard looks a guy like that would expect to get from a Deputy Sheriff of Clown-town, Michigan, and locked the car.

Arnie Halliday occupied three rooms on the twelfth floor. It was the usual set-up for a guy in that bracket. The outer office was staffed with the people who did the work. Then there was a smaller office, staffed by two efficient-looking women who probably carried the whole organisation. Mr Halliday was the last office among these barriers. I passed people, obviously waiting for a moment of the great man's time. They were young, old, anxious, confident, experienced, new, but all with a common problem. They needed the work. I didn't.

"Hey, you can't—"

One of the efficient lookers gave a startled yelp as I went past. I gave her a wide smile and said, "Watch me."

Arnie Halliday looked at his watch as I walked in.

"I'll give you one thing, Preston. You're prompt. Siddown, siddown."

He was fifty, on the fat side, tailored like the man in the ads. His face was bland and open, topped by well-nurtured gray hair. He didn't offer to shake hands.

"You're some kind of a sheriff, they tell me. I thought they went out of style when Ford started to operate."

I nodded.

"Around here, yes. But there's plenty of towns where the office still exists. Anyway, let's not argue about that. What I—"

126

He held up a hand for silence.

"Just a minute. Let us by all means argue about that. Now, who are you, and what do you want?"

The fact that Halliday was fat didn't mean he was soft with it.

"I'm a private investigator. It's a little matter of murder."

He leaned back, regarding me quizzically.

"And this sheriff thing, it's the bunk, right?"

"Oh no. That's true enough. Here."

I flashed the shield. He stared at it a long moment.

"But you're not here in that capacity. You're here as a private detective. Why all the big act to see me?"

I jerked my head towards the outer office.

"You're an agent. I could wait out there three days straight and still not get to see you. That kind of time I don't have."

Halliday grinned.

"Well, well. Maybe you are some kind of detective, at that. Something was said about murder?"

"One of your clients. An actress, Elaine Evans."

He pressed a hand against his head, and groaned.

"I thought I'd been through all that."

I poked an Old Favorite into my face and lit it.

"And what, Mr Halliday?"

He looked at me wearily.

"Look, the police have been on my neck ever since it happened. Especially one guy, from the Homicide Squad. Er—"

"Rourke?" I suggested.

"No, that wasn't the name. It was—er—Ranscombe."

127

"Randall," I corrected.

"Right. Randall. Big feller. Makes you tell him a thing ten times before he believes you. And then he checks it."

Gil Randall was not Mr Halliday's favourite person.

I chuckled.

"That's Randall, all right," I confirmed.

Halliday breathed noisily.

"Believe me, feller, there's not one damned thing I know about that girl that Randall hasn't got. He even made me remember things about her I'd forgotten I knew. Why are you here? Go talk to him."

I wagged my head sidewise.

"No can do. The lawmen don't like people like me too well. They don't have to tell me anything at all if they don't care to. And you'd be amazed how rude they can be."

He grinned briefly.

"I can imagine. Now, tell me about Elaine. Murder is strictly police business. Where do you come in?"

I flicked ash into a tray on his desk, and looked honest.

"Strictly speaking, Mr Halliday, Elaine Evans's death is no concern of mine. Naturally, I'm sorry it happened, but that's where my interest ends."

"In that case—" he registered puzzlement.

"There is another girl. Someone you never heard of. She came here some time back, and seems to have been a friend of Elaine's. Her family want me to find her, because there's been no word of her in months."

128

SOMEBODY HAS TO LOSE

The face across the desk brightened visibly.

"Ah, well now, maybe I can help you there. What's this kid's name?"

I shrugged in resignation.

"I don't know."

Halliday looked at me in disgust. I jumped in again quickly.

"No, wait a minute, don't misunderstand me. I know her real name, her family name, of course I do. But she wasn't using it here. And her relatives don't know what name she is—or was—using."

Halliday sighed.

"So now you need a girl with no name. I'd sooner deal with Ranscombe—"

"—Randall—" I corrected.

"—O.K. Randall. At least he knew what he was talking about and who he was looking for. A girl with no name yet."

He stared at the ceiling and waited.

"The point is," I began tentatively, "this girl often referred to Elaine Evans. On the telephone, in letters, that kind of thing. They seem to have been big buddies."

"And?"

"And I was hoping you may know something about Elaine's private life that could give a lead to this girl I'm interested in."

He snorted.

"Look, I'm an agent. I don't run people's private lives. I'll go further than that. I will tell you I make it my personal business to know not one damned thing about their personal business. Because this is a

S.L.—E   129

very big town, with some very big people, and it doesn't pay to know too much about what's going on. Elaine was a good kid. She did her work, she was reliable, she got paid. What she did on her own time was her business."

I nodded.

"That seems fair enough. So you wouldn't know about any men-friends or that kind of stuff?"

"Not a damned thing," he confirmed.

I had an idea.

"Tell me, without sticking my nose in your business, do you keep records of your client's work? You know, what the job was, how much it paid, what date, and so forth. Or is it simply an assignment comes in, you give it to George or Charlie, take your cut and that's it?"

A faint grin appeared on his not-unpleasant face.

"I don't know how good a detective you are, but you would make one lousy agent. Plus, you don't know much about the tax laws of our great nation." He paused to let me digest this, while I looked suitably puzzled. Then he went on.

"Listen, I have to keep a duplicate file system out there. One for the companies who come to me. Another for the people I represent. Both alphabetical. Plus, I have to have an accountant check both sets, once per month. This way the tax boys can't be cheated by three lots of people. One, the companies. They can't claim advertising expenses they didn't incur, because each transaction is logged in my system. Two, my clients. They can't claim they

130

haven't been working, because that's all on their personal record card. Three—"

I interrupted.

"You're three. You can't claim you haven't had the work or the clients, because it's all right there in the office."

"Check. So you see those b—" he checked himself, "those tax boys have it all buttoned up. Way I look at it, if they want all this information, I have to provide it. But to make me employ people just for their benefit, brother that rankles. Least they could do is supply the damned staff."

This was evidently one of Halliday's subjects.

"Mr Halliday, I wonder if you would object to my seeing some of those records?"

He squinted suspiciously.

"What for? How do I know you won't take a list of the companies then go to some other agent and tell him how much dough I'm making? It's been done before."

My turn to grin.

"You can have your staff watch me. If I start making lists they'll soon spot it."

He scratched a thoughtful chin.

"Well."

He flicked down a key on the office inter-com.

"Lucille. Come in here will you?"

The door opened almost at once. Lucille was one of the two in the middle office, the one who'd tried to stop me getting in.

"Lucille, this is Mr Preston. No, not just Mr Preston. Mr Deputy Sheriff Preston. He wants to have a look at one or two files—"

He stopped at the astonishment on her face, and chuckled.

"No, it's O.K. I think he'll want to see the Elaine Evans card."

Then he looked at me.

"Right?"

"Right."

"That may lead him to one or two others. There it stops. If you think he's getting too nosey, stop him, and report back to me."

"Very well, Mr Halliday."

I got up.

"Thanks for your time and cooperation, Mr Halliday. I don't think I'll be bothering you again."

He looked at me as though he hadn't been seeing me before.

"Say, you're a big feller. Not bad-looking. Neat dresser. You ever thought about acting or maybe modelling?"

I shook my head.

"No. Besides, I'd never get to shoot anybody."

He clapped his hands and laughed.

"I understand. Still, if your gun's ever empty, give me a call, huh?"

We shook hands and I followed Lucille outside. Without any preamble, she slid open a small drawer marked "A to E", and rooted around at the back. Out came a card with "Elaine Evans" in the top left corner.

132

This she handed to me, saying, "Here it is. As you see the date is in the first column, the time in the second, company concerned in the third. Column four is the fee for the assignment, and the last is a brief description of what's wanted."

"Lucille," I began, then paused. "Do you mind that? I don't know your other name."

She smiled. Some of the professional efficiency look was switched off. She had a pleasant face.

"No, I don't mind. After all, as Mr Halliday said, you are pretty big and not bad-looking. Lucille will be fine."

I smiled back.

"I was wondering, Lucille, why this card is still in the system? Everybody knows this unfortunate girl is dead."

She nodded.

"It's the law. We have to keep all these records for three years, dead or not."

I tried to look wise.

"Ah, yes, the tax authorities."

"No," she contradicted. "For them it's two years. This is for the Immigration Bureau."

"You get them, too?"

"Not regularly. With the tax people, we always know when to expect them. Regular schedule. But Immigration drop in whenever the fancy takes them."

Every day a little more knowledge.

"Well, I wouldn't have thought it. Do they ever trace anybody?"

Lucille wagged her head up and down.

"Oh, yes. In the six years I've worked here they have tracked down three people."

"Well, well," I well-welled.

Then it was time to look at the Evans record. She seemed to work with fair regularity, sometimes two or three assignments in one week.

"These fee entries," I asked, "would they be the fee for the job, or the amount actually paid to Miss Evans?"

"That is her fee. The agency deduction is taken before the entry is made."

"H'm."

A rapid piece of my inaccurate arithmetic suggested that Elaine had been pulling down between twelve and fourteen thousand a year. Not exactly a fortune, but not starvation level either. I turned my attention to the list of companies. They were mostly well known TV and radio companies, till I reached down to the last few entries. And then I took a deep breath.

In the two months before her death, Elaine Evans had carried out five assignments for Art-World. I could almost hear the rusty machinery clanking around in my head.

"Do you have a file on Art-World Incorporated?" I asked.

She grimaced.

"I had better have, or the tax-gatherers will start looking for their rubber hoses."

Lucille rooted around in another drawer. This time she came up with a regular file, in brown manilla. It seemed that Art-World were frequent customers. There had been several new entries since the Evans murder. I got one of my crazy ideas.

"Lucille, this probably isn't a fair question, because it's about something that happened a long time back. About eighteen months, if I remember. There was a girl murdered at a Hollings Street address. You wouldn't perhaps recall if she was a client here?"

She nodded vigorously.

"I should just say I do. We talked about nothing else for weeks. As a matter of fact, just the other day I was saying," she hesitated, and looked almost shy.

"Yes, go on Lucille, what were you saying?"

Encouraged, she continued.

"Well, of course, I'm nobody's Deputy Sheriff, but I said it was a big coincidence that Gloria and Elaine both seem to have died the same way."

"Gloria?"

"That's right. Gloria Stafford."

"And she was a client here, too?"

"Yes. It was a terrible thing to have happened."

I wasn't really listening. I was poring through the Art-World file. It was there all right.

Gloria Stafford had worked for Art-World seven times immediately prior to her death.

I passed back the file.

"Lucille, you may not care too well about keeping all these records, but believe me you have saved a tired old detective a great deal of time and work."

She smiled her thanks.

"If there's anything else. Anything at all?"

Pretending I didn't know what she meant, I

replied, "I won't hesitate to come back. Thanks again."

She was standing holding the file and getting a good view of my broad, manly back as I went out.

12

I FINALLY located a pay-phone where they hadn't ripped out the coin-box and called up the house manager of the apartment block where Elaine had been living.

"Who is this please?"

"This is Deputy Sheriff Preston. I am investigating the murder of Miss Elaine Evans."

His voice was plaintive.

"But I have already told the police everything I know. Absolutely everything," he insisted.

"I don't doubt that, sir," I told him placatingly. "Just rounding out my file. Tell me, what was the rental on the murdered woman's apartment?"

Now he was tetchy.

"Rental? Oh, well, I have it someplace. Hold the line."

I passed the time reading one or two interesting messages which had been scribbled on the walls of the booth. He came back.

"Are you there? Oh. The rental was seven thousand dollars per annum. Of course, it was dirt cheap what with prices and all. The next tenant will have to—"

"Yes, I understand. Thank you, sir, for your time and trouble."

I cradled the phone, and tapped at my cheek. Then I dialled Monkton City police headquarters, and asked for Sergeant Ben Fawcett. Ben heads up the Vice and Morals Squad, and we'd worked on a couple of things.

"Fawcett."

"Ben, this is Preston."

Pause.

"What kind of a Preston would that be?"

"Abraham Washington Preston," I told him. "You know, there's a homicide somewhere in town, Rourke can't find any suspects. So he always says, 'Get Preston'."

He chuckled.

"Oh, that kind of Preston. How are things, Mark?"

"So, so. Look, it's nearly half-twelve. I imagine even you flatfeet are entitled to a few minutes for lunch?"

"On occasion," he returned guardedly, "what's it all about?"

On Vice and Morals, a guy gets more offers than any other section of the force. They get involved in every kind of vice and graft there is, and the operators would as leave not be disturbed. So they make offers.

Money, girls, vacations. An officer on that particular squad has to be very careful of what he does. I could understand Fawcett's caution, even with me.

I laughed.

"Tell you the truth, officer, this is a kind of corruption offer. If you meet me in Sam's place in ten minutes, I will buy you one glass of beer and one sandwich. That should be good for fixing a morals rap, wouldn't you say?"

"O.K. Ten minutes."

I was holding a dead phone.

*   *   *

At that hour, Sam's was beginning to liven up. There was the usual crowd. Newspaper people, horse-players, business guys. I elbowed my way to the bar, and signalled to Sam, who was filling up beer glasses as fast as his huge shoulders could pull. He saw me, and pointed to the beer. I nodded, and he separated one from the rest.

"Hi, Mr Preston. No time to chat today."

He gestured at the thickening crowd.

"Sure, that's **O.K.** Sam. Say, I have a friend coming in. Can you get a couple of ham sandwiches filled?"

"Sure thing."

He took a five dollar bill, made change, hollered through a hole behind the bar, and got back to mining that beer.

I was early, and thus able to indulge one of my favourite bar pastimes. Nasty-minded people call it eavesdropping, but I prefer to think of it as gleaning information. There were three characters behind me, obvious movie people, and they were discussing how Davis Ronald got the second lead in Fall of the Gladiator. I was beginning to warm to this Ronald when I felt a light punch on the arm.

I turned, and there was Ben Fawcett. He was just as good-looking as always, thirty-five years old, and his eyes went through you like a laser beam.

"Something was said about beer," he mentioned.

I waved to Sam, who knew my visitor at once. Two fresh beers were laid in front of us.

"How about those sandwiches, Sam?"

"Should be about ready. I'll check it out."

Clutching our beer and sandwiches, we looked around for a place to sit. Luckily for us, Sam's is a stand-up and hurry kind of place at that hour. People don't go there to sit around and dawdle. It's in, drink, eat, talk, and out.

There was a small table in one corner, about big enough to survive the ashtray that was placed in the centre. I put this on the floor as we sat down.

"Prosit," said Fawcett, dipping his nose in the beer.

"Skol," I returned.

I watched the shining teeth disappear into the double-decker.

"H'm," he muttered, between chews. "Pretty good. I could maybe get you off with twenty years, if you cop a plea."

I grinned at him.

"You don't know yet what the rap is."

He wagged a finger.

"For sandwiches of this class, the rap is not important. Still, since you mention it, why all this champagne and caviare?"

I lit an Old Favorite, and studied him through the smoke.

"I just thought maybe we could talk a little, push the ball around. I need some information."

He put a hand in his pocket, pulled out a tube, unscrewed the cap and squeezed it over the sandwich.

"Mustard," he explained. "Always carry my own. Can't trust these places. Sometimes they don't supply it. Even if they do, there's always some comedian who swipes it. Carry your own, that's the secret. What kind of information?"

I knew I had to select my words with care. All this comedy, with the beer and the double-decker and the mustard, did not make me forget for an instant that I was sitting with one very smart copper. He would probably hate to do it, but he would put me away if he thought I was the wrong side of the line.

"There was a girl murdered last month. Elaine Evans."

Fawcett shook his head.

"You're wasting your money on all this high living. I don't mess with homicide. That's for Rourke."

I ignored this. Keeping my voice low, I said, "It might be more your business than you think. Now, this Evans was registered with the Halliday Agency—"

Again he shook his head.

"Halliday is O.K. I had him checked out more than once. No call-girls, no fun-parties. Nothing like that. Strictly legit."

Well, I'd learned something already.

"There's more. I've been checking on the Evans girl. She worked mostly on radio and TV. Small stuff. Just before she died she had a number of jobs with one special outfit."

He wolfed the last of his sandwich, studying me carefully before he spoke.

"So?"

"So there was another girl, name of Gloria Stafford. She was pretty much like Evans, small-time actress, model and so forth. About eighteen months ago, she was murdered in circumstances very similar."

Fawcett shrugged irritably.

"Look Mark, I'm kind of a busy copper. This is all Rourke stuff. Go tell him."

"He already knows," I assured him. "Not much the Irishman misses."

"That's for sure. So where do I come in?"

"I don't know that you do," I confessed. "But this Stafford was working for the same outfit that Evans was, just before she was killed."

"And?"

"And this is where you might come in. I hear some funny stories about an outfit called Art-World Incorporated."

He stopped in mid-swallow and stared.

"I'm a guy likes funny stories. Tell me yours."

I could feel I wasn't wasting my time.

"Mind, I'm no expert. I just repeat what I'm told."

"So what are you told?" he said impatiently.

"I'm told this is a big money operation. I'm told they make terrible movies about monsters and fiends

142

and space-ships and you name it. These movies are used as program-fillers where the corn is tall. But I am also told the outfit has a little side-line. They make different pictures, the kind that would interest Vice and Morals. And that's where the big money comes in."

He pointed at my sandwich.

"Don't you want that?"

"Not much. I'll eat later."

He nodded slowly.

"The public. You guys can eat anytime you feel like it. Now if you were a working copper—"

He left it lying. I picked it up.

"I am, in a way. Just I don't have a uniform. About Art-World?"

He munched and chewed and looked thoughtful.

"How much do you know?" he demanded, spreading mustard.

I told him about Stillman, I told him about Laurel and Hardy and the guy who called himself Grover J. Mitchell. The baronial hall that passed as Mitchell's pad, not forgetting the gorilla who guarded the driveway.

By the time I was finished, so was the sandwich.

Fawcett said, "Just one question. I appreciate all this steak and wine and stuff, but what makes all of this any of your put-in?"

Luckily, I'd been waiting for that one. I looked annoyed.

"Any of my put-in?" I retorted. "Do you realise I have been questioned over a murder rap? On top of that I've had guns waved in my face, been ab-

143

ducted, frozen half to death, scared out of my wits. My put-in? I want to get back at somebody."

He listened to this outburst with a solemn face. When I was through, he thought for a moment, then his sides began to shake in silent mirth.

"Preston, you are the most. People have been showing you guns, scaring the pants off you, most of your life. It never has bothered you before. What's all this cream-puff act suddenly?"

This was the reaction I'd expected, and indeed relied on. I cracked a small grin.

"Well," I admitted, in my candid, open way, "I was thinking that somewhere in all this jungle, there has to be a little reward money for something."

He was tuned in now.

"Ah."

He sounded satisfied.

"So why should I help you pick up reward money, for a lousy sandwich?"

"Two," I corrected.

"O.K. Two. It's pretty hard for a simple copper, watching people like you scoop up the gravy when we've done all the work."

I inclined my head.

"I can understand how you feel, Ben. But look at it this way. There are people around getting away with murder. There are times when you boys know who they are. But because of the law, because of regulations, police procedure and so forth, there isn't a damned thing you can do about it. That's when a character like me can be useful."

"You mean you break the law?"

144

"No. I mean I act as an individual. I don't have to report to anybody. I am not bound by a procedure manual."

I lit an Old Favorite for the umpteenth time. It tasted like uncured seaweed.

Fawcett breathed heavily.

"Trouble is, I kind of halfway trust you. It's a great sign of weakness in a cop."

I grinned at him.

"Wrong. You know I'm better than half-way honest. That's more than you could say for fifty per cent of the guys in this bar right now."

He nodded morosely.

"O.K. Maybe I will tell you a thing or two. This Art-World outfit, it's a real pain in the ass. You're right about the kind of pictures they make. But you have to catch them doing it. I've tried, Lord knows. Also, there's some kind of blanket on the show. I've never been able to pin it down, point any fingers. But raids get cancelled, people I want to talk to high-tail for Mexico, or Cuba or whatever. Nothing I can point to, but it's there."

The policeman licked reflectively at a spot of mustard in the corner of his mouth.

I took a deep breath.

"Is it really the outfit, Art-World I mean, or is it someone in particular you want?"

Fawcett looked pained.

"Someone in particular? Where have you been all these years? Of course I don't want someone in particular. What is this, a Western? I'm just like any other copper. I need a nice offense, a nice piece of testimony, a nice genuine guilty party, and one nice conviction."

He spread his hands in that nice convincing way I have learned to distrust over the years.

"So who is it?" I asked.

"Who is it?" he groaned. "How can an honest man make a living in this town, when nobody believes anything he says? But I'll tell you this, Preston. There is a who."

Ah. We were beginning to make conversation.

I crushed out the half-smoked cigaret.

"Do we know who is the who? Could it be for instance somebody who runs an outfit called Art-World Inc?"

Fawcett took another pull at his beer. All the time we'd been together, the glass wasn't yet half-empty. Well, I reflected, if they ever pinned anything on this guy, it wouldn't be alcoholism.

Now he wiped off some foam, and sneered at me.

"Two points," he stated. "One, if I knew the who, I'd be out there chasing all over the city, till I had him pinned down. Two, I wouldn't be wasting my time, boozing it up with every private eye in town."

I chuckled.

"Two points," I replied. "One. We have been here twenty-five minutes. You have not yet drunk one half of that beer. That makes you kind of inefficient at boozing-it up. Two. There really is somebody. Right?"

His good-looking face became serious.

"I think there has to be. Whether it's your candidate, I don't know. Let's not name any names. I know the guy you're talking about. Could be. But I don't know it. And," he paused for emphasis, "let's be clear about this. I'm not playing coy and hard to get. Your man is on my list, but he's not the only one. This isn't one of those deals when I know damn well it's so-and-so. Not like that at all. But there is somebody, and if you help me turn him up, maybe I'll buy the sandwiches some fine day."

It was my turn to look serious.

"Well now, Ben, I don't know. When I buy the grub, you eat all of it. What chance would I stand if it was your treat?"

His face creased into a great grin.

"You realise I have to report our talk to Rourke?"

"Why not?" I retorted. "They have to keep tabs on big lunch-time boozers like you."

He rose, sucked noisily at his beer, still failing to empty the glass.

"Tell you what I'll do," he offered. "If I hear anything that may help you to help me, maybe I'll tell you."

Not a bad deal for a pair of sandwiches and a half-glass of beer. A promise from Fawcett was money in the bank.

"Likewise," I said.

He grinned.

"Similarly."

Personally, I prefer my cops illiterate.

13

I GOT to the office around one-thirty. La Digby was presenting a very square back to visitors today.

"Oh, hallo, Miss Digby. You managed to fix up that little matter?"

She turned and regarded me coldly.

"That little matter, Mr Preston," and the "little" was heavily underlined, "that little matter has been seen to. Could you spare a moment in your private office?"

I could. I most certainly could.

In my own room, I made a point of not taking a chair, until I was sure Florence was safely seated.

Then I parked and said, "Where is she?"

"The address is on your desk, Mr Preston."

She was right, it was there, in front of me.

"How was she, when you left her?"

148

"About as I would have expected. Nervous, worried." Florence regarded me severely. I tried to remember what I'd done that was wrong. Without success. "You see, Mr Preston, there are a few people left in this world who are afraid of murder and general mayhem. People who don't like guns and knives and—and—" she cast about desperately "—and bombs and so forth."

I was tempted to ask what the "and so forth" represented, but I resisted temptation. Instead I said, "Sure, I understand. But she's in no danger that I know of. Only you and I know where she is. And even if other people know, I can't think why they would want to harm her."

She looked at me hard.

"Well, if you're sure."

"Sure, I'm sure," I was sure. "If she gets into any trouble, it won't be for lack of effort on my part."

Florence was mollified. Somewhat.

"Naturally, I'll be guided by you, Mr Preston."

Inwardly, I sighed with relief. If Florence stopped trusting me and got worried enough to go to Rourke, I'd be facing those high gray walls.

"Believe me, I already have fresh information about all this. It should take maybe two, three days to jell."

I didn't have much faith in my words, but as it turned out I was short-changing myself.

The phone rang. Florence went for it instinctively.

"It's a man," she announced. "He wants you. Sounds rather upset. He won't tell me his name."

I was thoughtful as I took the receiver.

149

"Preston."

A man breathed heavily at the other end.

"This is Roy."

Ah. Now what would he want with me.

"O.K. Roy. What can I do for you?"

His voice was urgent.

"Look, Preston, I've got what you want. Bring one thousand dollars with you, and it's yours."

"Just a minute, while I check my billfold."

Florence watched the pantomime curiously.

"As of now," I reported, "I have one ten, three fives, seven one-dollar bills, and some change. That amounts to, let me see—"

"Stop horse-playing around," he butted in. "The banks are open. One thousand. I'll give you an hour."

This guy was in trouble.

"Look, Roy, you're not giving me anything. What you mean is, you reckon you have about one hour to get out of town, out of debt, or whatever. What you mean is, you need the thousand. Don't do me any favors."

A pause while he thought about it.

"Listen, Preston, you could be right. Maybe I could find myself in a jam, if I don't scram outta here. Maybe I do need the lousy grand. But that don't mean I'm peddling trash. This merchandise I'm talking about, believe me it's worth it. In fact, it's worth a lot more, but I don't have the time to go shopping around."

I stared at the phone.

"Look. I don't know what you have. Even if I did know what you have, I don't know that it's of any

150

value to me. Even if I knew that, I don't know that it's worth one thousand dollars." As an afterthought, I added, "Always assuming I have one thousand dollars."

There was a short interval. Then he said, "Preston. What I have would net you one hundred grand minimum in the cheapest game in town. Plus it will tell you something about the accident to the late Stillman."

I pushed the receiver against my cheek and tried very hard to concentrate. This would have to be it. The missing treasure. The sea-chest bit.

Grover J. Mitchell had said there was something of the kind.

"Listen, Roy. It will take a little time to dig up the money."

"Like what kind of time?" he demanded.

"Like about two hours," I told him.

There was a pause while he thought about it.

"And no cops," he said finally.

"No cops. Where'll I find you?"

He told me the name of a small coffee-shop out on Avenida. It was a forty minute drive.

"O.K. Here's the set-up. I come alone. I find you alone when I get there. If you've got company, I start blasting the minute I step through the door. And all I get from the law is medals. Am I getting through?"

He sighed noisily.

"Aw, come on, Preston. What is this, the Brick Radford show? What time'll you get there?"

I told him, and we hung up.

151

The Digby had difficulty in controlling her curiosity. In the ordinary way, I would have left her dangling. But seeing she'd been such a help with Louise, I gave her a break.

"Well, Miss Digby," I announced importantly, "it seems we may be able to throw some light on this matter."

She actually registered animation.

"And that poor girl? She may be safe?"

I looked important.

"Well," I hesitated, importantly, "one can't be positive, but I think this is a step in the right direction. On the practical side of life, the first thing is a thousand dollars in cash."

I put that "we" in there to illustrate that Flo and I were in this thing together.

It's doubtful whether Florence Digby ever fluttered in her entire life, but she was close to it now.

"What do I have to do?" she queried.

"Get me the head cashier at Farmers and Trustees. Tell him I need a thousand dollars in used fives, tens and twenties, and that you'll be down there in fifteen minutes to pick it up."

She didn't exactly snap to attention, but her whole attitude was conditioned by the war pictures. If she'd said, "Yessir, lootenant," it wouldn't have surprised me. What she did say was "I'll get it right away."

Which was almost as bad.

*　　*　　*

I turned onto Avenida, looking for a slot. This is

SOMEBODY HAS TO LOSE

not a busy part of the city, not in daytime anyway.
I parked a few yards from my destination, and was
careful about locking the car. Then I marched into
the grimy interior of the coffee-shop, peering around
for my man. At the same time I was trying not to
look like a guy carrying a thousand dollars in used
bills. In this neck of the woods there were people
who'd skin you alive for your pocket handkerchief.
There weren't many customers around, and Roy was
not included.

"Hey, mister."

Behind the counter a large man beckoned to me.
He was beautifully dressed in a gray undershirt,
topped with an apron advertising the tools of his
trade. Like coffee stains, tomato sauce, bacon fat and
other delicacies. He evidently enjoyed his own cook-
ing, tipping the scales at two fifty plus.

He leaned across confidently as I approached. I
wished he hadn't done that, because his breath
matched up to the apron.

"You look like a guy who's looking for a guy," he
offered.

"Could be," I returned guardedly.

He nodded.

"There was a feller here, said he was waiting for
somebody. He wouldn't tell me any names, but he
gave me a description. You're the one all right."

"So where is he now?"

The counter-man became all confidential again.

"Well now, he gave me five to pass that along.
He seemed to think you'd spread another five to hear
it."

153

I might have known.

"O.K." I laid five in front of him.

A hand like a side of bacon closed over it.

'He's out at the park. You know, they have these cages with all these colored birds locked up? Personally I don't think it's right. Them little birds don't have no right in cages. Birds is meant to be free. If you ask me—"

I cut in on him.

"You are absolutely right. I'm thinking of starting a campaign to stop all that kind of thing."

His face brightened.

"Yeah? Well you can rely on me to back you up, mister. I mean, what kind of life is that for those pretty things, cooped up all day so kids can poke sticks at 'em?"

"Right again," I assured him. Imagine there being a heart somewhere in all that blubber. "Something about a message?"

"Eh? Oh, sure. This guy said he'd be around the tropical bird area."

"Thanks."

I turned to make for the door.

"Hey."

I looked back. He wagged a finger the size of a baseball bat.

"Don't forget now, you need names on one of those lists, you know—"

"—Petitions?" I suggested.

"Right. You bring it to me."

"Got it."

As I climbed back into the Chev I was wondering

why Roy had changed his mind. Or maybe he hadn't. Maybe he never intended to stay in the cafe, but only to ensure I would turn up.

I drove slowly out to the park, and walked over to the aviary.

A large mynah bird looked at me with evident interest, as I strolled by.

"Hello," he said.

Startled, I turned and looked at him.

"Hello yourself," I replied.

It was all the encouragement he needed. It was evident he had once belonged to a seafaring man, and I checked quickly to ensure there weren't any children within hearing distance.

"Tut-tut," I reproved. "You should be ashamed."

As I walked away he rattled off in what could have been Chinese, though doubtless the content was the same. A bird with a varied history obviously.

I saw Roy in the distance. He was admiring a bunch of brightly colored birds of varying species, all from South America.

"Hello Roy."

He spun round at my voice, and the relief on his face was evident.

"Thank God it's you."

"Who else would it be?"

He shook his head.

"Not important any more. Did you bring the money?"

"Yes. But I still don't know what I'm buying," I reminded.

155

One thing was certain. He wasn't toting any sea-chests today.

"Let's find a bench and siddown."

This was not the urbane, groomed character I'd seen before. This man was ashen-faced, rumpled and nervous.

We found a wooden bench that was empty. A shrill noise announced the arrival of a school outing, led by a grim-faced woman who was going to have no nonsense. I hoped the mynah would remember his manners.

"Preston, I'm in trouble."

That much I'd already guessed.

"What kind of trouble?"

"Big trouble, murder trouble."

I watched the kids for a moment, munching pop-corn and emptying coke-tins.

"About Stillman. Did you push him over?"

He shook his head.

"No. I don't even know who did it. But I think I know why."

I fidgeted.

"You know, Roy, plenty of people would like to know why. But I don't think the why is worth a thousand bucks. What we really need is the who."

"Look, I have this information. Once you have it, you'll know it has to be one of a few people. From there you can operate."

Sudden shrieks of delight distracted me for a moment. The school-kids had located the mynah.

'That bird," I remarked irrelevantly, "uses words I haven't even heard since the Navy."

156

"Never mind the goddam bird," he snapped, "let's stick to business."

I looked at him mildly.

"O.K. But you haven't told me what our business is. All I know is you want one thousand smackeroos American, and I don't know what it buys."

He looked around anxiously, to be certain there weren't people with tommy-guns hiding in the inch-deep grass all around.

"Stillman was a blackmailer."

"A good reason for being knocked off," I agreed. "But there would need to be more."

'There is. In his desk at the club, he always kept one drawer locked. I didn't worry about it. Maybe it was emergency cash, personal stuff. None of my business, anyway."

"So?"

He paused.

"I'm taking an awful chance with you, Preston. You could take what I've got, not give me the money, then I'm no place. Right?"

"Right."

I set fire to an Old Favorite, and looked at him.

"What you say is right. But remember two things. One, whatever you have may really not be worth the money, in which case I won't give it to you. Then there's two. If your merchandise is worth the grand, and I double-cross you, I'll spend the rest of my life waiting for you to put a bullet between my shoulder-blades. And, unless I'm a poor judge of character, you are a guy who would do exactly that."

He grinned wolfishly.

157

"You're right about that part. But don't worry, this stuff is worth the money."

I exhaled smoke. The mynah was now doing his Chinese act again, to the evident disappointment of his audience. Except, that is, for the much-relieved lady teacher.

"Something about a locked drawer?" I prompted.

"Yeah. Well, when I find old Barney, I have to think fast. I'm supposed to keep him alive. There's gonna be people who don't like me letting him get dead that way."

"Unless those people took care of it themselves?" I suggested.

He shook his head.

"No, they wouldn't operate like that. If Barney had to go, I would have had the phone call."

That made the kind of sense that prevails in Roy's world. Who better placed to knock off the boss than his own bodyguard?

He started talking again.

"So I looked at him, and I'm in trouble. It wasn't my fault, but they'd make it my fault. Then there was the cops. They'd be looking for a patsy, and I'm made to measure. What I needed was out. And fast. I searched Barney's pockets. Nothing there, just a few hundred bucks. I took most of it, left the rest so they couldn't shout robbery. But I did find his keys."

Now we were back to the drawer.

"I thought of the drawer. Maybe there'd be more dough in there. So I unlocked it. I was wrong, but in a way I was right."

158

I clucked impatiently.

"Come on, Roy, this isn't guessing time. What'd you find?"

He slid a hand inside his jacket and pulled out a small leather-bound book. It was about the size of a pocket diary.

"This."

He handed it over.

The cover was plain, tooled red leather with gold art-work around the edges. I opened it up. The first page bore the inscription "With the compliments of Art-World Enterprises". The following pages were hand-written, and each contained the name of a girl, home address, telephone number, general interests. And vital statistics. A girlie service, not so unusual in our fair city. I didn't find it very interesting. I'd seen things like it before.

I looked at Roy and shrugged.

"I don't get it," I admitted.

"Keep turning."

It was certainly interesting to know that Charmaine had a forty-two inch bust, and that Lydia offered unusual services, but it didn't seem to be getting me very far. Again I shrugged.

Roy repeated, "Keep turning. You give up too easy."

I made a mental note about Angela, and was quite intrigued by the alleged prowess of an oriental lady, but I just kept turning the pages, as instructed. Then I found her. Gloria Stafford. And the page had been criss-crossed in ink.

Red ink.

A few pages later, there was another name, new to me, and with an L.A. address.

Jill Hyams.

And more red ink.

I knew now what I was going to find if I kept looking. Halfway through the book, and there she was.

Elaine Evans, plus red ink scratches.

Roy watched me anxiously.

"Well, what do you think?"

I stared at the cages. There was a large evil-looking parrot whose sole ambition seemed to be to bite off any unsuspecting fingers which protruded through the wire mesh.

Finally, I said, "We seem to have a book. A book about girls who can makes themselves available for fun and games. At a price. Three of them have been murdered. I didn't get to hear about the Hyams case by the way?"

I made it a question. Roy shrugged.

"Neither did I. But those addresses in there are not exclusive to Monkton. Why would we hear about just another killing in the six or seven cities covered in that book?"

"True."

But there was a common factor. Whoever originally owned the book knew about the L.A. killing as well as the two in Monkton.

"Roy, I can see this is a valuable document. The police can do a lot with it, both Homicide and Vice and Morals. But I don't see it gets me anywhere. Not one thousand dollars worth of anywhere."

He snorted.

"For a cop, even a private cop, you're not very thorough. Look at the back cover."

Neatly embossed in gold lettering was the legend

PRESENTED TO EDWARD F., CARRINGTON

I stared at it in disbelief. Roy chuckled.

"Now you see why I have to blow town. I can't fight Carrington, the political machine, Art-World and the cops, all rolled into one. Somehow or other I'd wind up with one to five, even just for having a dirty shirt. No, I need that grand, and a fast train."

I looked at him, sliding the little book into my pocket.

"One last thing. How do I know you didn't hit Stillman yourself?"

He sneered.

"If I'd hit him, you'd know. I'm a heart and head man. All that stuff in his chest. He could've stayed alive for hours. Amateur night."

True enough.

Reaching inside my coat, I pulled out a fat buff envelope.

"It's all there. Used notes. Travel far."

He stood up, pocketing the money.

"You made a good deal," he assured me.

Then he turned and walked quickly away.

On my way out, I stopped by the mynah's cage.

"Arrividerci," I told him.

He didn't know any Italian, and contemplated me with silent fury as I made for the car park.

14

I WENT to the office. If I'd been nervous about carrying a thousand dollars in cash, I was positively jittery about the small potential lump of gelignite now in my pocket.

Miss Digby was out somewhere. Probably fussing over Louise.

On my desk was a note.

> "A Mr Harris telephoned to say that you should bet a horse called Bad Girl in the five o'clock race at Palmtrees."

It was an omen. Just the other day I cleaned up on a nag called Naughty Woman. Now here was this Bad Girl, which was coincidence enough in itself, but when you added in the stuff I had in my pocket, well, it was obviously rob-the-bookies day.

162

I phoned Keppler and put one hundred on the nose.

"Look, Preston, where do you get all this information?" he demanded. "That dawg was sold to a glue factory two years ago, and you know what? The factory refused it."

"Don't make life hard, Julie. One hundred."

He grumbled again and hung up.

I sat moodily chewing on a cigaret. There was no question about what had to be done. My problem was the sequence. Finally, I made up my mind to do it right for once, and picked up the phone, dialling. At once a gruff voice said, "Monkton P.D."

"Put me on to Lieutenant Rourke, will you?"

"Who's this?"

I told him who's this, and he said to wait, there was a clicking, then the irascible Irishman said, "Listen, Preston, I have work to do."

"Nice talking to you too, John," I assured him. "I have something for you, but I want Randall or Schultz with you when I hand it over."

He didn't like that.

"What're you afraid I'll steal it?"

Seriously, I replied, "No. As a matter of fact it's as much for your protection as mine. You'll understand when you see it. Fifteen minutes O.K.?"

He grunted something that might have been assent and hung up.

The desk sergeant hardly looked at me when I walked in. I'd been in the place so many times he probably thought I was on the force.

163

"Rourke's expecting me," I told him, making for the battered stairs.

I knocked on the dirty glass partition and went in. Rourke was behind his worn desk, facing Randall behind the other.

"Come in, come in," he greeted. "Where's the stolen jewellery?"

I parked on the rickety chair provided to remind visitors they weren't supposed to stay too long.

Rourke looked across at his sergeant, who shrugged.

"I have something which may well help you solve two murders in this city, and possibly a third in Los Angeles. I want you to have it, and fast, because I think carrying it around is like carrying a bomb. In return, I want something."

The grizzled Irishman groaned, spreading his fingers on the desk-top.

"He gives me bombs and asks favors. Well, I might as well hear it."

"I want you to give me four hours clear, no tail, then I'll come back here if you want, and stay all night."

"Why would I do anything for you?" he demanded.

"Why would I come in here of my own free will, and solve all your problems for you?" I countered.

He looked at Randall, whose nod was imperceptible, if you didn't happen to be accustomed to Randall's imperceptible nods.

"I need your word you are not criminally involved in whatever this is."

"You have it."

164

"Well, all right. Four hours. Am I allowed a stenographer now?"

I wagged my head sideways.

"Not yet. Hear me out, and you'll realise it may not even be in your own best interests for too many people to know right now. When I said bomb, I meant bomb."

He didn't like it, and shifted on his chair.

"It better be good. Get on with it."

I lit a weed, and tried to lean back. The chair warned me to lean forward again.

"It starts with a man named Edward F. Carrington."

If they'd needed waking up, that did it. They were so interested, they didn't even interrupt.

"Carrington has a daughter. She's over twenty-one, kind of headstrong. She took up with a night-life character who was on vacation or something over in Waldron City. When he came back here, she came with him. He was Barney Stillman."

"Ah-h."

They said it together.

"She wasn't using her own name," I continued. "Carrington wanted her found, and he hired me to do it."

"Why you?" Randall wanted to know.

"You're not going to like this. Carrington wanted the best there is. He was told I'm it."

Rourke snorted.

"Why would a smart guy like that believe fairy-stories?"

"Do you want to hear this, or not?"

He shrugged and shut up.

"I got lucky. I found the girl in record time, because some comedian pinched her backside out at the track. There was a fight, and that led me to Stillman."

"How?"

This from Rourke.

"He was in the fight. The girl was with him. It was her derriere that started it."

"O.K. Go ahead. The assumption seems to be that Louise Carrington was this Louise Russel they talked about at Stillman's joint?"

"Right."

Randall began filing his nails.

"O.K. So you found her. What then?"

I stubbed out the butt.

"Then I got paid, and it was over."

Rourke gave one of his great theatrical groans.

"Preston, we are very busy men. Out there," he waved towards a window encrusted with tobacco smoke, "Out there, the people believe we are working day and night to preserve law and order in this remote village. They wouldn't believe it if anybody told them we spent all our time yakking it up with every lunatic who happens to walk in here. If there is a point, which I begin to doubt, will you get to it?"

I thought a slightly hurt look was indicated. Rourke wasn't the only actor around here.

"I had to tell you all that to fill in the background," I said stiffly. "Of course there's a point, and I'm coming to it. There was a man, kind of house

166

manager out at the Green Parrot. Name of Roy something."

"Roy Baedeker," supplied Randall. "Eleven arrests, two convictions. Strong-arm, protection, assault with a deadly weapon, you put a name to it, he's done it."

He leaned forward eagerly.

"It was Baedeker who shuffled old Barney off. That's what you came to tell us?"

I looked pained.

"Why don't you pay attention when I tell you things? I told you I was carrying a bomb. If I came to tell you one hoodlum rubbed out another one, I wouldn't make all this fuss. Matter of fact, I don't really have an idea about who pushed old Barney over."

Randall began to expostulate, but Rourke waved him down.

"All right, Preston. Now you've got us all excited, get it said."

I looked like a man controlling his ruffled feelings.

"This Roy, he called me up today. Said he'd found something. He wanted a thousand dollars for it. I was to meet him."

"And?"

"And I met him. What he'd found was a little book. A book filled with girls' names. Plus addresses, phone numbers, and type of service on offer. Roy was scared. This was the big league, and he didn't think he could buck it. He wanted out-money."

Rourke looked sceptical.

"And you gave it to him?"

"You can check with my bank. I drew one thousand dollars in bills of small denomination this afternoon."

"Uh-huh. Why?"

"Because that's what he asked for."

Randall's turn to groan.

"That's not what we mean, Preston, and you know it. We mean, why would you invest a thousand dollars of your own money in something which is none of your put-in? Or do you happen to have a source which will refund your little investment?"

I hesitated.

"I have a client who left money with me. I used some of that."

Rourke lit one of his Spanish cheroots.

"You're going to be mighty popular with this client. Who is it?"

"I'll tell you that when I come back."

He didn't like it, but under state law I don't have to reveal the name of a client under certain circumstances.

"Huh," this from Randall.

"Mark, I think you're wasting our time. The names of a few girls, some telephone numbers. What's in it for us? Sounds like Fawcett."

This was my moment of drama. I took out the little leather book and placed it in front of Rourke.

"There are three names in there, scratched out in red ink. Gloria Stafford, Elaine Evans, and a girl named Jill Hyams from L.A."

Rourke snatched it up, riffling at the pages. His lips pursed in a silent whistle.

"Look inside the back cover," I prompted.

He did so and stared without belief at the inscription.

"Jesus!" he said softly.

Randall was almost jumping up and down with frustration. Rourke took pity on him and tossed the book over. Randall turned the pages quickly, making grunting sounds as he did so.

"Wow!"

The Irishman turned his cold eyes to me.

"I don't get it. This little item is worth a lot of money. Opposition newspapers, television companies, Carrington himself. Any of those would empty the safe for this. Why come to me? I couldn't get you five dollars out of the Police Fund."

I shook my head sadly.

"You know me, though you pretend not to. Like now. I'm no shakedown artist. To me, this is important evidence in two, probably three, murder cases. The place for that kind of stuff is here."

There was silence while they thought about that.

"Edward F. Carrington," muttered Rourke. "This could turn the whole state machine upside down. Too big for me."

Picking up a telephone, he barked, "Get me the Commissioner. That's right, the Commissioner personally. I don't care if he's at a meeting, or playing golf, or what. I want him now."

Putting down the phone, he stabbed a finger at Randall.

"Get Schultz to check this Jill Hyams thing with L.A. And then get back in here."

"Check."

169

We sat, trying not to look at each other, till the big sergeant came back.

"This lid will blow in less than one hour. Let's try a little police work," suggested Rourke. "You say you got this bomb—yeah, I agree with you, it's a bomb—from this guy Roy?"

"Right."

"So why didn't he keep it? Why not blackmail Carrington? He could have ridden that old gravy train the rest of his life."

I shook my head.

"No. It was too big for him. He's a small-league man. I think he probably kept the book a few days, dawdling around with thoughts like that. But he's not a fool. He could never buck the big action. So he got out."

"Maybe."

Rourke crushed out his black weed.

"Now if this Roy found it, it means Stillman had it before. You think Stillman was, as you put it, bucking the big action?"

"Seems a fair assumption," I returned carefully. "And he is in the morgue. No assumption there."

The door opened and Schultz came in. He looked at me.

"O.K. to talk?" he asked.

"Sure, sure. Preston knows all about it."

Schultz nodded.

"I've talked with L.A. They had this Jill Hyams case about four months back. She was butchered, and I mean butchered, in her apartment. You know,

170

Lieutenant, it sounded to me a lot like this Evans case we have on the books."

Rourke groaned.

"I was afraid it would. Thanks."

As the door closed behind Schultz, the phone shrilled.

"Rourke. Yes, Commissioner, I know you have a tight schedule, but this won't wait."

There were sounds of noisy expostulation at the other end. Rourke waited for the noise to die away.

"Sir, I have three homicides, and there's a strong political tie-in."

This time there was a pause of several seconds, before the other voice spoke again.

"Yessir, you heard me correctly. A very big man is involved. This one is too much for me. I want it on your desk, and fast."

More silence. Then, "Thank you, I'll be at your office in one hour."

He put down the phone.

"By tonight, unless we can figure some way to keep this under wraps, which I doubt, the whole town will be on fire. I want you, Preston, back in this office by ten o'clock. I'll keep my end, no tail, but you be here."

I got up.

"Don't forget who brought in the book."

Outside it was steamy. The cool evening breeze from the ocean had not yet started in business. I drove down to Sam's for a cold beer and a quiet think.

I knew whatever I did was going to be wrong.

Roy had the right idea. Don't buck the big action. But I've been doing just that all my life. People get too old to change.

I called the *Globe.* Steiner was not too pleased to hear from me.

"Look Shad, a favor," I pleaded. "There's twenty bucks riding on this."

"An honest working stiff can't afford wagers. What's it about?"

I told him, and he said to hang on, so I hung on, and finally he came back with the answer.

"But I get ten per cent," he added.

"Right. I'll deposit two dollars with the fund for destitute reporters."

Next I called a Wiltshire number.

"I want to speak with Grover J. Mitchell. And before you start building the barricades, tell him the name is Preston. Mark Preston. If Mr Mitchell knows what's good for business, he will see me in exactly thirty minutes."

I waited while the lackey went to see the great man. It was a long five minutes before he came back.

"Mr Mitchell will be pleased to receive you, Mr— er—Preston. Thirty minutes."

I made fast time out to the Mitchell hovel. The guard had a good look at me and waved me up the driveway. The car park wasn't doing much business today. I dumped the Chev and began marching towards the house.

"Hello."

A man's voice. Turning, and shielding my eyes against the early evening sun, I spotted Mitchell stretched out beside the swimming pool. He seemed to be alone.

He was a man who had little time for the simple life. Next to him was a trolley covered with bottles, ice-buckets, olives, you name it.

"You are prompt, Mr Preston. Always a good sign. Help yourself to a drink."

I settled for Old Angus, about four fingers, and dropped in some crushed ice. You had to hand it to the guy. He looked good. Flat stomach, good tan, exuding good health.

"Something was said about business," he reminded.

The Old Angus was hitting the spot. I pulled up one of those beach-side chairs and parked.

"I have some information which can save you a lot of pain and anguish, Mr Mitchell. You'll know about it tomorrow anyway."

"So why bother to tell me today? If it's bad news, I'm in no hurry to hear it."

I leaned forward.

"But with me telling you one day ahead, you can make certain arrangements."

"Ah." He picked up a tall glass which looked as though it contained Bacardi on the rocks. "And of course, you will require money."

"Of course."

He nodded ruminatively.

"How much money?"

"Five thousand dollars."

Mitchell regarded me quizzically, a slow smile spreading.

"You really are a most engaging fellow. I took a

liking to you the last time we met. Now you want five thousand dollars for something I can read in tomorrow's papers."

I shook my head.

"Wrong. I want five thousand dollars for something that doesn't have to be in tomorrow's papers. The something is you."

"Ah." He regarded me carefully. "And why should you do me this enormous service?"

"For five thousand dollars," I told him.

He laughed. Not a cynical laugh, not a chilly laugh, but a genuine belly-rumbler.

"Preston, I believe we are going to have our talk. Let us go into the house."

I followed him across the patio, and into a large cool room. It seemed a pity to leave the drinks-trolley behind, but I needn't have worried. There was a fully-stocked bar.

He stretched himself out, motioning to a chair.

"Fire away."

It was no time to pull punches.

"You make yak pictures, just this side of the censors. You also make other pictures, which nobody can prove. The Vice and Morals squad of Monkton P.D. are very interested in you."

He yawned.

"I can scarcely be blamed for the inflamed imaginations of a bunch of flat-footed policemen."

"O.K. Now, in these pictures you use youngsters, unknowns. They have contracts which hold water. No work, no eat. So you find them other work. It pays well, they eat. You circulate the names of suit-

174

able people to prominent citizens who can afford to pick up the tabs."

He smiled, and sipped at his drink.

"You can prove all this, of course?"

I set my glass on a small walnut table.

"You've been unlucky, Mitchell. Haven't you noticed in life, that no matter how carefully you plan everything, there's always something, some stupid oversight, some person who doesn't come good at the right time?"

"The best laid schemes," he murmured.

"Right." I was gambling now. "About the little red books."

He really did look surprised this time.

"Books?"

"Yes, you know, you present them to prominent people, and then supply information as to what entries might interest them. You even have their names embossed in gold."

"Keep talking." He was no longer so calm.

I set fire to a cigaret and took a pull at Old Angus. Let him sweat.

"I've seen one of these books. Bad luck for you, I agree, but the guy you gave it to took it into his head to murder three of the girls. Three. And you recommended those three."

He swallowed the Bacardi fast. Too fast. Then he stood up and made himself a large refill.

"All right, so you have the book. Deposited with a lawyer, who will take it straight to the Police if anything happens to you. It was five thousand, wasn't it?"

175

I laughed at him, and meant it.

"You know, Mitchell, you're rich. You're really rich. Do you think I'd come here with a penny-ante trick like that? Five grand. P'shaw. For that kind of transaction, I should need one hundred thousand dollars."

He was getting agitated.

"Five thousand dollars is one thing. One hundred is an entirely different matter. You're talking in riddles."

"I'll make it plainer. I'm giving you a few hours start. When I tell you what you need to know, and believe me, you need to know, you'll have all of tonight and most of tomorrow to straighten things out. You see, the lid is about to blow, all over the state."

He smiled weakly.

"Come now, that's a bit dramatic."

I agreed with him.

"Yes, it is. But it's true. You haven't asked the name of the man inside the book. It's Edward F. Carrington. And the Police have the book."

Mitchell slumped back in the chair. Under the tan, his face was ashen.

"It can't be."

"But it is. Now, I'm sure you're going to be a busy man. You have to cover up, get lawyers working. You might have twenty-four hours, but you can't even count on that. Think yourself lucky that you have some warning. Your first move is my cheque. Five thousand dollars, and it's a steal."

He staggered, rather than walked, to a side table, opened a drawer and scribbled.

"Five thousand."

I took the piece of blue paper and examined it.

"You're lucky," I told him. "I probably saved you one quarter of a million dollars, and seven to ten in the penitentiary on charges of moral corruption. But there is one more thing."

He was deep in thought. He shook his head and said, "What?"

"One more thing. Who killed Stillman?"

A helpless shrug.

"I don't know. None of my people. I thought at first it was Roy, but that was a dead end."

Oddly, I believed him.

"Well, time's getting on, and you have a lot to do. I'll see you."

There was no sign of Laurel and Hardy as I saw myself out.

15

I CHECKED Louise's address from the chit I'd slipped into my pocket. It was a fifteen minute drive to a pleasant tree-lined neighborhood. I pressed for Apartment 6A, and the door clicked open. I walked around until I found the right door. Some work on the buzzer and then her voice.

"Who is it?"

"Preston," I assured her.

There was a lot of bolt-sliding and lock-clicking, then the door opened one half-inch.

"Oh, Mark, I've been so—so isolated. Come in. Come in."

I came in. She was lovely as always, looking a little strained, which was not surprising under the circumstances.

"Can I get you something? Some coffee, a drink?"

I thought about what I had to say to her.

178

"I'll take a drink, if you'll have one." As she made for the kitchen, I hollered, "Make it two large ones."

I was quite certain I needed a stiff drink. With what I was going to say, I thought she would, too.

When she came back she was holding two frosted glasses. They looked good. We sat down, and she smiled.

"You know, I don't believe I've ever felt so—so—"

"Isolated?"

Louise giggled. She was getting more relaxed every minute. Now.

I took a hefty pull at the drink.

"Roy had the book," I told her.

"But he—"

She stopped quickly, but she should never have started.

I looked at her sadly.

"That's all wrong, honey. You should have said 'what book?'"

"Well, of course, I haven't the faintest idea what this is all about."

I sighed, and put down the glass.

"It's about a little book your father had. It contains details of the girls he used to visit on his nights out. It also includes three girls he probably murdered."

Her face was white.

"You must be mad. Why, my father—"

"—Is a man," I finished. "He visits girls. Lots of men do. They don't all find it necessary to kill them as well."

"You don't know my father," she spat. "He's a fine man. He wouldn't—"

"—Then why was he paying Stillman blackmail money?"

She bit her lip.

"Have you got it now?" Her voice was low.

"No. The police have it. Within a few hours they'll have your father as well."

Louise stood up, livid with rage.

"They wouldn't dare," she stormed. "Why, my father's done more for this state, this whole country, than any living man."

"He's killed three women," I stated flatly. "He has to go over. There isn't anybody so important he can get away with that kind of stuff. Is that why you came here with Barney in the first place?"

She dropped her gaze, and her voice was low.

"Yes. I thought if I was close enough to him, sooner or later I'd get my hands on the pocket-book. It didn't work."

I shook my head, and finished the drink.

"You know, you're a strange one, Louise. You knew what your own father had done, yet you tried to cover for him. What makes you set yourself above the law? Who do you think you are?"

"The name is Louise Carrington, spinster. Note the name. We have been leading this country for three hundred years, Mark. And the man happens to be my father. Do you know something? I don't even feel guilty."

I nodded.

"Not even about murdering poor old Barney?"

She did a double-take.

"Barney?"

180

"Sure, Barney. Mind if I help myself to another drink? I'm not enjoying this too well."

Out in the tiny kitchen, I located the fixings, and made a big one. When I got back inside, she was sitting with her hands clasped in her lap.

"Tell me about Barney."

She wagged her head around.

"I don't know what you're talking about."

"It was you." I made it a statement of fact. "At first I thought it could have been Roy. Other things happened that ruled him out. Then I thought it might have been some blue-movie outfit, but that didn't jell either. Tonight, I thought it could have been your father, Lord knows, he had reason enough. So, I checked him out. He was in San Diego on one of those talk-in TV shows. That leaves you."

"This has to be a bad dream. You rule out these gunmen and criminals, and then assume it's me?"

I sat down, grateful for the drink.

"One of the gunmen and criminals made a very good point to me lately. The shoddy way old Barney left this world. The actual words were 'amateur night'. And there's something else."

She looked up then.

"It had to be somebody he trusted. Somebody who knew the rear way in. And remember, he didn't even have a gun in view."

"That proves nothing," she blurted out. "Why, anybody could have sneaked in the back way and—"

"—shot old Barney in the back of the head? True, but nobody did. Somebody stood in front of him,

181

SOMEBODY HAS TO LOSE

somebody he trusted, and blew holes in him from five
or six feet away. You were that somebody."

"What're you going to do?"

I looked surprised.

"Do? I'm going to turn you in, that's what."

She clutched at her skirt.

"Listen, Mark, I'm a wealthy woman."

"Good, then you can afford the finest legal advice
on offer. Shall we go?"

I got to my feet. She stared at me in dumb disbelief.

"You mean, you intend to go through with this?"

I nodded.

"It's a question of murder, Miss Carrington. You'll
probably get off with a parking ticket."

*   *   *

Down at headquarters I found a subdued Rourke
and Randall, and a very under-subdued Police Commissioner. He rounded on me as I walked in.

"It's about time," he snapped.

"No it isn't. The deal was for ten o'clock. It's only
nine thirty-five."

"Don't get uppy with me, Preston. What're you
trying to do, put the whole Carrington family behind
bars?"

I looked at him without love. Bringing Louise in
had given me no pleasure at all.

"If that's where the whole Carrington family
belongs."

There was a tap at the door and a uniformed
officer poked his head around.

"I said no, positively no, interruptions," snarled the Commissioner.

"Yessir, I know, but I thought you should have this."

"This" was a folded sheet of paper which the officer passed over.

The Commissioner read it, tight-faced.

"All right."

The officer scuttled out.

There was a heavy silence, a police station, special kind of silence.

The Commissioner went to the window. I wondered why. You couldn't see through it.

Finally, he turned.

"There's been an accident. Ed Carrington was cleaning a hunting rifle. He didn't realise it was loaded. He died instantly."

Snow job.

"As for you, Preston, you've been in this office making all kind of wild accusations against a fine citizen. I need not tell you, I never want to hear a whisper about it again?"

I sighed with resignation. It pays to know when you're licked.

"Right. Maybe I was mistaken."

Rourke broke what was for him an unusual non-speaking period.

"There's still the girl."

"Ah. Yes, the girl."

The Commissioner tapped at his forehead with the 'accident' report.

"Well, of course, we haven't seen any evidence yet.

183

From what I hear, she's a strong-willed young woman. It'll probably turn out that the man Stillman attacked her, and she had to defend herself. Something of that kind. Anyway, there's no point in my staying here now. I'll be on my way."

After he'd gone, the two policemen studiously avoided looking at me. I got up.

"Well, there's not much point in my hanging around. We don't seem to have any business. Think I'll go and tie one on."

Rourke looked at me, heavy-lidded.

"Mark?"

"Sure, John. I know."

I closed the door gently.

16

A FEW hours, or was it a few months later, I rolled into the office. Florence Digby was normally frosty, but today she was glacial.

"I've been listening to the radio," she told me.

"Oh really? How'd the Buffaloes make out?"

She sniffed. When La Digby sniffs at you, you know you've been sniffed at.

"No doubt you think that's very funny, Mr Preston. As a matter of fact, I wasn't referring to the Buffaloes. How could you do it?"

I tried not to look guilty.

"I don't know what you're talking about, Miss Digby. And I need a drink of water."

I went through into my own office and attacked the water cooler. Outside, the city went about its business as though nothing had happened. It always did. My old fantasy came back to mind. The one where I go to bed for ten years, and when I finally emerge nothing has changed. Except maybe the street signs are different, the taxes are higher. No. Correction on the second part. No maybe about that. The taxes will definitely be higher.

The door behind me opened, but I went on staring out the window. At the busy street, the traffic. Anything.

Florence's voice pierced my shoulder-blades.

"Mr Preston."

I'd known this would be coming, and I turned reluctantly.

"What is it, Miss Digby?"

She stood there, immaculate as ever, groomed and cool-looking, whatever the sun might be doing outside.

"Mr Preston, I have worked for you for a long time."

It was a statement of fact, which called for no answer. I inclined my head.

"In all that time, I have had a number of unpleasant experiences. I have received threatening letters, anonymous telephone calls. People of criminal character have called in here. Police officers have been rude to me, believing I was covering for you. In fact, they have quite often been correct."

She was obviously waiting for a comment.

I said, "We both know what you say is true, Miss Digby. What point are you making?"

For her, she seemed almost flustered.

"Well—er—well, in all that time, I have tried to

186

be loyal. I have seldom asked you questions. It has been my belief that what you do is for the best."

I looked at her carefully. This could be an important conversation. The Digby had been like another right arm to me for many years. I hadn't seen her this way before. It was as though at least part of the impregnable shield, which always surrounded her, had been lowered.

"I like to think that, too."

It was like talking to a stranger.

"Miss Digby, won't you sit down for a minute?"

She sat, or rather perched, stony-faced. Then she blurted out, "But she was such a splendid person. So straight-forward, so sincere. Believe me, I know something about people, especially women. There isn't a bad bone in that girl's body. If she did what they say she did, she must have been driven to it. She must have—"

"Hold on, Miss Digby," I cut in. "It so happens I agree with everything you say—"

"—Well then—"

"—but," I bored on, "the fact is, she killed a man. He may not have been much of a man, but he was entitled to live. I am not concerned with people's motives. That's for others to worry about. Lawyers, juries, court-rooms. If I start setting myself up in the judgement business, I'm putting myself above the law. Now, I may cut a few corners now and again, if it seems the right thing to do. That's a chance I take, and the law doesn't mind too much, if they think I'm being honest overall. But once I know someone has committed murder, I don't have any choice about what to do. It's out of my hands, I have to turn them in."

She sat very still, staring at the wall.

There was a long minute of silence, while I watched my cigaret-smoke spiral towards the ceiling.

Finally, she said, "When I came in here, it was to resign."

That was what I was afraid of. I kept quiet.

"However, listening to you, I can see you are right. I still don't like it, but if we are to have any law, we can't have people setting themselves above it. But I hope that girl goes scot-free, law or not."

I shrugged helplessly.

"And I shall remain," she finished.

A snort of relief would have been out of place.

"I'm very pleased to hear it, Miss Digby. I believe we've sort of gotten used to each other over the years."

She looked up now, and gave me a faint smile.

"Yes, I believe we have."

When she reached the door, she said, "Oh, there was a telephone call. A Vale number. Someone called to say there were no hard feelings from Mr Laurel and Mr Hardy."

I chuckled.

"Well, that's a relief. Thank you."

She went out, closing the door.

On the desk, next to the small pile of mail, rested a neatly folded newspaper. I suddenly remembered

188

my bet with Keppler, and turned to the race results.

Bad Girl had not been lucky.

They seldom are.

* * *